To Dee Dee,
May God shower you with blessings,
Barbara Warren

Hidden Danger

by
Barbara Warren

HIDDEN DANGER BY BARBARA WARREN
Published by Lamplighter Mysteries
an imprint of Lighthouse Publishing of the Carolinas
2333 Barton Oaks Dr., Raleigh, NC, 27614

ISBN: 978-1-946016-17-1
Copyright © 2017 by Barbara Warren
Cover design by Elaina Lee
Interior design by Karthick Srinivasan

Available in print from your local bookstore, online, or from the publisher at:
lpcbooks.com

For more information on this book and the author visit:
http://www.barbarawarrenbluemountainedit.com/index.htm

All rights reserved. Non-commercial interests may reproduce portions of this book without the express written permission of Lighthouse Publishing of the Carolinas, provided the text does not exceed 500 words. When reproducing text from this book, include the following credit line: "*Hidden Danger* by Barbara Warren, published by Lighthouse Publishing of the Carolinas. Used by permission."

Commercial interests: No part of this publication may be reproduced in any form, stored in a retrieval system, or transmitted in any form by any means—electronic, photocopy, recording, or otherwise—without prior written permission of the publisher, except as provided by the United States of America copyright law.

This is a work of fiction. Names, characters, and incidents are all products of the author's imagination or are used for fictional purposes. Any mentioned brand names, places, and trademarks remain the property of their respective owners, bear no association with the author or the publisher, and are used for fictional purposes only.

All Scripture quotations, unless otherwise indicated, are taken from the Holy Bible, New International Version®, NIV®. Copyright ©1973, 1978, 1984, 2011 by Biblica, Inc.™. Used by permission of Zondervan. All rights reserved worldwide. www.zondervan.com. "NIV" and "New International Version" are trademarks registered in the United States Patent and Trademark Office by Biblica, Inc.™.

Brought to you by the creative team at Lighthouse Publishing of the Carolinas:
Marisa Deshaies, Managing Editor
Meghan M. Gorecki, Publishing Assistant to the Managing Editor
Jennifer Harshman, General Editor
Judah Raine, Lucie Winborne, and Christy Distler, Proofreaders

Library of Congress Cataloging-in-Publication Data
Warren, Barbara
Hidden Danger / Barbara Warren 1st ed.

Printed in the United States of America

Praise for *Hidden Danger*

Barbara Warren has earned a reputation for grabbing her romantic suspense readers with a nice shock from the start and maintaining interest until the ending. Pick up this book and you won't ever want to put it down.

~**Hannah Alexander**
Author of the Hallowed Halls series

Ms. Warren had me hooked with the fast-paced opening in *Hidden Danger*. A strong plot and building tension had me burning the mid-night oil. Great story!

~**Lori Copeland**
Author of *Amelia and the Captain*
from Harvest House Publishers

A heart-stopping, breath-taking tangled web of deception and intrigue. Warren's mysteries leave no room for competition. *Hidden Danger* is an all-nighter.

~**Bonnie Engstrom**
Author of *Natalie's Deception*,
Number 5 in the Candy Cane Girls Series

Warren's world feels like Everytown, USA. We relate to her characters and believe the dangers they face. I'm seriously considering installing an alarm system after reading *Hidden Danger*.

~**Prix Gautney**
Author of *Season of Crows*

Barbara Warren is a published inspirational romantic suspense author who writes exceptional stories. Her books leave you on the edge of your seat, anxiously turning pages and wondering what will happen next. She does a great job of keeping your interest until the very last page of her books.

~**Jeanie Smith Cash**
Author of *Peonies on an Amish Quilt*

In *Hidden Danger*, Barbara Warren takes the reader on a compelling journey filled with suspense and intrigue. From the beginning I was hooked. Who doesn't love a military hero and a strong heroine? Carley and Blake delivered both.

~**Breanda Minton**
Love Inspired author of the
Martin's Crossing series

ACKNOWLEDGMENTS

My thanks to Susan Eschbach, Matthew Eschbach, Linda Sartin, Sherrie Akers, Prix Gauntney, Carol Parscale, and Ronica Stramel for the great job they did critiquing this book. And a special thank you to my agent, Linda Glaz, and to editors Marisa Deshaies and Jennifer Harshman for all their hard work. I appreciate you all very much.

Dedicated to my family, the one I was born into and the one I married into. I love you all and appreciate you so much.

Chapter One

Carley Sutherland drove through Silver Oaks Park, gripping the steering wheel and darting nervous glances at each side of the road. A crescent moon peered dimly through misty clouds. Shadows created deep pools of darkness beneath the looming trees.

The hair on the back of her neck prickled. Why had Nancy chosen this creepy site for a meeting place this late at night? How could anything be so important and hush-hush it had to be discussed in a place like this? Carly would never drive through here at night if she had a choice, but her best friend's voice—frightened and shaking—dispelled any inclination she had to stay at home and watch TV. Carley couldn't turn her down. She'd never been able to say no to Nancy, which was one of the reasons they had been in trouble so often when they were younger. They were too much alike. Actually, she'd been a little wilder than Nancy, but they were both too quick to act first and think later. Although they were of no blood relation, they were as close as sisters.

She spotted the car up ahead, Nancy standing by the driver's side as if ready to jump in and take off. The rigid outline of her shoulders and the tightness of her expression in the glow of the car lights warned Carley that this wasn't a casual meeting. Not that she had really thought it was.

She parked and got out, hurrying to meet her friend. "Are you all right?"

Nancy slumped against the car and shook her head. "I'm in big trouble."

"What's wrong?" How could anything be this bad? From somewhere in the darkness, an owl hooted. Carley shivered at the sound.

Nancy motioned toward a park bench a short distance away. A streetlight from somewhere up ahead shed a dim glow. "Let's sit out in the open so I can hear if a car is coming. You didn't tell anyone I'd be here, did you?"

"No, of course not." Why would it matter if she had? What was Nancy running from? Because it was easy to see she was scared out of her mind. And that was unusual. Nancy didn't scare easily. The park at night had never bothered *her*.

It wouldn't have bothered Carley, either, back when they were younger, but her life had changed. Now she was more cautious, more aware of what could happen. She and Nancy had been friends since grade school—back when they were both cheerleaders and everything was right with their worlds. A lot of troubled water had slithered under the bridge since then.

She sank down on the bench and Nancy slumped beside her, so close their handbags mashed between them. Carley's eyes had adjusted to the dim light, and she could see her friend's hands shaking with whatever fear had driven her to the park tonight. Her lips quivered and tears glittered on her lashes.

Carley pulled her into a hug. "What's wrong? Tell me."

Nancy's lower lip quivered. "I stopped at The Old Mill restaurant two nights ago. The place was deserted except for a man and woman across the room from me, but close enough I could see something was wrong. They were arguing and then the man jumped to his feet and jerked her out of the booth, almost dragging her out the door. She looked back at me, like she wanted help, but I didn't do anything. What *could* I do?"

"Nothing, I guess." Apparently it had been a private argument.

Nancy drew a deep breath that ended in a sob. She sucked in her lower lip as if fighting for control. "He was too rough and I could tell she was frightened. So I did the only thing I could think of. It was just an impulse, but I grabbed my phone and took a picture of them. From the way he glared, I think he might have seen me. I looked out the window and saw him shoving her into a black SUV. He circled around and drove past my car."

She dug out her phone and started searching through it. "At lunch today, I saw the same woman on TV. She'd been found in a ditch on a back road outside of town."

Carley's mouth dropped open. "Rachel Blevins? I saw that. You think she was the woman at the restaurant?"

"I know she was. I got a good look at her when they left the restaurant, and I recognized her on the morning news. And I have this picture of her. I had to leave early to go to a meeting out of town, and all day I've felt creepy, like someone was watching me." Her breath caught on a sob. "On the way back tonight, someone in a black SUV tried to run me off the road—where there's that steep dropoff—right before I got to the bridge. I'm sure it was him. Who else would have reason to tail me like that? I'm afraid to go home. Afraid he'll be waiting for me."

"Why didn't you come to *my* house?"

"I didn't want him to see my car there and drag you into this. This area of the park is so secluded, and it's usually vacant this time of night, so I thought if we met here he wouldn't know and you could help me decide what to do."

Carley raked her fingers through her hair, grabbed Nancy's shoulders, and said, "It's possible this guy is a killer, so the first thing you need to do is tell the police."

"I will, but I just need to talk to you. Need to calm down and pull myself together." She brushed her trembling hand across her forehead. "I'm so upset I can't think straight. If I'd gone off the road there, I'd..."

At the drone of a car motor, Nancy shoved the phone into her purse and jumped up. Carley jerked around to see headlights flashing through the trees, then stared at her friend. "Nancy? What's wrong?"

"It may be him. Carley, don't let him find me."

Before Carley could do anything, a dark SUV pulled alongside the park. The window rolled down and a gun barrel emerged through it. Something dark covered the driver's face ... a mask.

A gunshot ripped the air.

Nancy fell.

Carley leaped erect, stumbled, and dropped, her knee striking a rock. Pain surged through her. Fighting to gain traction, she lunged to her feet, purse in hand, and made for the trees. A second gunshot exploded. A bullet smacked into a large oak in front of her. Bits of flying bark stung her face. She tripped, recovered, and plunged down an incline, desperate to get away.

A car door slammed. Footsteps pounded after her.

Pain stabbing her knee, Carley zigzagged through the darkness, dodging trees and bushes. She gasped for breath. *God, help me. Please! I don't want to die. Not like this!*

Blake Richards jogged through the park the way he often did when sleep eluded him. When memories of too many nights spent listening to the sounds of battle kept him awake. The park was usually deserted this time of night, which suited him. And the Missouri Ozarks were a world away from Afghanistan.

Gunshots exploded, the sound all too familiar. He dodged behind a tree and dropped to his knees. Sweat speckled his forehead. He gasped for air as memories clouded his mind.

Forcing himself to his feet, Blake rose, standing in the shadow of the large oak tree as footsteps crunched in the dry leaves. A woman darted through a patch of pale moonlight, heading his way. Blake hunkered down until she got close enough to grab. One arm went around her waist, the other around her shoulder as he clasped his hand over her mouth to keep her from screaming.

Her body twisted frantically, lunging to break free. He gripped her tightly against him, whispering in her ear. "Hush. I'm trying to help you. Let's get away from here."

His car was parked at the rest area below them. He pulled her down the slope, trying to stay in the deepest shadows. Someone ran across the blacktop road behind them, footsteps slamming against the pavement. The woman stumbled in the dark and Blake caught her, half carrying her to his car.

He opened the passenger door and shoved her inside before running around to get in, praying all the while she wouldn't leap out and bolt. "Are you all right?"

"*All right?* After what just happened? No! Who are you?"

"The guy who saved your life." He drove off the road in a half circle, swerving to go back the way he had come. A gunshot blasted from somewhere behind them as he stomped the gas, surging down the road.

Blake flicked a glance at the rearview mirror before concentrating again on driving. No sign of car lights following them, but he wanted to get away from there as fast as he could.

The woman beside him gasped out something he didn't catch.

"What?"

"Nancy… He shot Nancy."

"Who's Nancy? Who shot her?"

"I don't know. He just drove up and shot her." Her voice trembled, and he hoped she wouldn't fall apart. He had enough to deal with without a hysterical woman on his hands.

Blake wanted to ask what she was doing in the park at that time of night, but there was something he needed to do first. He fumbled in his pocket for his phone, dialed 911, and gave the dispatcher his name, location, and what details he could. The dispatcher took Blake's statement about the shooting in the park, asked him a few questions, and ended the call. Blake concentrated on his driving, checking the rearview mirror to see if anyone was tailing them. They were approaching the outskirts of town when the woman beside him spoke again.

"Where are we going?"

"Someplace safe. That guy seemed to want you awfully bad."

She'd been sitting with her face turned away, watching the side mirror—probably checking for car lights like he was and wondering if they were being followed. He hadn't gotten a good look at her yet. Not that it mattered. He had more important things on his mind.

Blake's phone rang and he answered to find Russ Pryor, Chief of Police and a friend of his, on the line. "Where are you?"

He glanced out the window at the street signs. "On Old Scott Road, just passing Walmart."

"We found the woman. She's dead." Something in his voice seemed odd, a little off-center. If it had been anyone else, Blake would have said he sounded shaken, but not Russ Pryor. It would take a lot to shake him. Still, the way he clipped his words seemed to indicate he was more disturbed than he wanted to let on. So what was going on? He wanted to question Russ, but that could wait. It might be best to talk privately.

"I see." Blake kept his voice casual, not wanting to upset the woman sitting beside him. She was stressed enough and he didn't have time to deal with overwrought emotions.

"She still with you?"

"Yeah."

"Okay, I need to talk to you both. I'm on my way to the station. Take her there."

"Got it."

Russ ended the call and Blake took his eyes off the road long enough to whip a quick sideways glance at his passenger, who still had her head turned, looking out the window. Funny, she seemed familiar, but he had too much on his mind to concentrate on that. A glimpse of blond hair swinging down to touch her shoulders in soft waves wasn't enough to remind him of who she could possibly be. He'd been away from Westfield too long—college and then the army. A car pulled out in front of him and Blake slowed, watching the road and checking the rearview mirror again. "That was Russ Pryor. He's a cop. They checked out the crime scene."

"I know who Russ is."

He hated to tell her the rest, but she'd soon find out the truth. Maybe it would be better coming from him than the police. "Your friend is dead. Russ wants us to come to the police station and tell him what happened."

She was quiet—too quiet. Then she muttered, "All right. I guess we don't have a choice."

They drove the rest of the way to the station in silence. Blake parked and turned to face his passenger, stunned when he recognized her once he was no longer distracted by the adrenaline of escaping a madman. He sagged against the seat as if someone had punched him in the gut.

Carley Sutherland.

Still the prettiest woman he'd ever seen. Blond hair shining like silk under the glow of the streetlight, eyes the blue of a summer sky. He'd always been attracted to Carley when they were younger, but back then he'd tried to steer clear of her, figuring she was headed for trouble and he couldn't afford to get involved. So how did he end up with her in the passenger seat of his car? God must have a sense of humor.

"Carley? Are you okay?"

What he meant was, what are you doing involved in something like this? Then again, considering that she'd been more than a little on the wild side in high school, maybe it was just the sort of thing she would be mixed up in. Judging by the madman who had just killed her friend and chased Carley through the park, she hadn't changed much, and for some reason, that bothered him.

She glared at him. "No, I'm not okay. How do you think I feel, running away like that and leaving Nancy behind?"

"There's nothing you could have done to help her, and running is the only thing that saved you."

She frowned at him. "And that should make me feel better? I abandoned my best friend. I kept thinking maybe she was just injured. Maybe I left her alone to die."

Blake held his hands out as he turned toward her. "You said there was a man with a gun. Don't blame yourself for what happened. There wouldn't have been anything you could have done to save Nancy."

Blake thought back to their days at Westfield High School. Nancy? Probably Nancy Wilkins, Carley's best friend in school and her partner in crime. Not that they'd done anything criminal that he knew of. It was just that if anything happened, the two of them were usually in the middle of it. His mother had been a teacher at the school, and he'd been careful not to do anything that might have caused trouble for her. A widow doing her best to raise a son and a daughter wouldn't have needed her son causing problems at her place of employment.

He opened the car door. "Let's go inside and get this over with."

She walked alongside him and he realized the top of her head reached the bottom of his chin. He caught a faint whiff of her perfume. Blake jerked up his thoughts, not willing to go there. Even if he wanted to get interested in a woman, this wasn't the right time.

As soon as he received his orders, he was going back to Afghanistan. He'd been wounded once. It could happen again and the next time might be a little more permanent. He'd seen too many of his buddies die, leaving wives and family behind. He couldn't ask a woman to wait, not knowing if he would come back or not, or what shape he'd be in if he did. Better to wait until he was home to stay before taking on any emotional entanglements.

Blake held the door open for Carley and followed her inside. He'd try to help her with whatever was going on and hopefully not get his heart involved too deeply—which would be difficult, considering the feelings he already had for her.

Carley glanced around, not sure what to do. Blake stood beside her, tall and competent. She resisted the urge to move closer to him, not sure how he would take it. Not sure how she would feel, either. Realizing the man who had saved her was Blake Richards had jolted her almost as much as being shot at.

She hadn't seen Blake since they'd graduated from high school. Actually, she never had seen much of him. They hadn't run with the same crowd. She'd liked to have fun and he was more serious, involved in church. Something she hadn't been interested in back then. Funny how her world had changed. Church had become an important part of her life.

Blake had matured, of course, but she could also see a hardness in him, a strength he hadn't had when he was younger. She'd heard he was home from the army, recuperating from being wounded in Afghanistan, but she hadn't run into him around town. His dark hair was cropped short, but his eyes were just like she remembered, a warm golden brown. Carley remembered a lot of things about Blake Richards, particularly that he was the one boy in Westfield she could never attract, no matter how hard she tried. Oh, he'd always been friendly enough, but that was it.

He had deliberately avoided her in high school, which probably caused her to pursue him. The challenge. She'd never had a problem getting any boy she wanted. Any boy except Blake Richards. He was the last person she expected to end up in the police station with on the second to worst night of her life.

She knew Russ too, of course. She had gone to school with him and they'd always been friends, but as he ushered them into an office, he seemed different. His lips were tight, his movements stiff, and his eyes flared with anger and something else she couldn't quite understand. No one had shot at *him*, so why was he so upset? Russ' gaze centered on Carley and she suddenly felt nervous, although she didn't know why.

They sat down and he stared intently at her for a minute before shoving a hand through his hair, rumpling the thick brown locks. His hazel eyes were guarded, watching her. "You all right?"

She nodded, not sure what to say.

"Why were you and Nancy in the park this late at night?"

Carley took a deep breath that was almost a sob. "Nancy asked me to meet her there and she sounded upset, so I agreed."

"Ah-huh. What did she want?"

She didn't want to talk about this. The memory was still too fresh, too raw.

Hidden Danger

It was all she could do to force out the words as she repeated what Nancy had told her.

"She thought he was after her?"

Carley gripped the purse in her lap and brushed at dirt on her jeans, trying to collect her thoughts, to remember every detail, to help Russ find out who this killer was. She looked down at her hands, trying to swallow the lump in her throat. "That's right. She started to tell me more, but a black SUV drove up and she tried to hide. He shot her but when he shot at me, he missed. I ran away through the park, and then Blake found me and brought me here."

"Why didn't she come to us instead of you? That's what the police are for." He still sounded angry and Carley guessed she could understand after all. He used to date her best friend, and it had seemed serious until Nancy caught him cheating. Russ had become depressed and angry after they broke up. Carley liked him, and she used to hope he and Nancy could get back together. They seemed right for each other.

Carley was angry at Nancy's death too. From what Nancy had said, she only took a photo of the argumentative couple as people in the restaurant. Now, she was dead. Carley had lost her best friend. The one person who had stayed with her through the good times and the bad. It wasn't right. Nancy was too young to die. Shot down—no way to defend herself. Carley wiped her eyes. The image was burned into her mind. She would never forget it. She couldn't.

Carley tried to appease him, although she realized nothing she said would help. Blake sat in a chair beside her, and just having him there, strong and calm, was comforting. "She had an out-of-town meeting and had to leave early. The way I understand it, she didn't know about the woman found in the ditch until noon. The place where she ate lunch had the television on, and Nancy recognized the woman then and realized she was dead. And then someone followed her and tried to run her off the road."

"But why you?"

"She was scared. Needed to talk to someone. We've been best friends since grade school. You know that. She would have come to you when she calmed down, but she didn't have a chance. He just drove up and shot her." Of course Nancy came to her. Carley would have done the same.

Russ stared at her for a minute, his gaze hard and unforgiving. She wanted to demand he explain why he was treating her this way, but before she could say anything, he turned his attention to Blake. "What were you doing there?"

Blake shrugged. "Sometimes I have trouble sleeping, so I go for a jog in the park. I heard a shot and stopped to investigate. I found Carley."

Carley remembered clearly how roughly he had grabbed her, almost causing her heart to stop, before hustling her down the slope to his car. She'd had no idea who he was.

"So neither one of you saw anything that would help us?"

Russ sounded frustrated, and something more, but Carley couldn't grasp what was wrong. She didn't blame him for being upset, and if she knew anything else, she'd tell him. She wanted this man caught. "I wish I had gotten a look at him. Nancy didn't deserve this. She didn't have a chance."

Russ nodded, his expression stern. "We'll do our best to find him. We checked out your car and left it at your house for you. Here are the keys. Blake, can you drive her home? I'd send a policeman with you, but we've had a four-car accident wreck out on Highway 57 plus this thing with Nancy. I'm shorthanded right now."

"Sure, no problem. It's on my way."

On his way? Carley struggled with an irrational surge of irritation. She wouldn't want him to go out of his *way*, for goodness' sake. And someone could have at least asked her if she wanted to ride home with him. After all, she was sitting right there.

Russ stood. "Thanks for coming in. We'll be in touch."

She followed Blake out to the car and got inside, more than a little upset. "Do you know where you're going?"

"You still live on West Sunshine?"

"Yes. The same house." She was surprised he remembered. They'd never been that close even though he used to live a couple of streets behind her. In fact, his mother still did. Was he staying there?

It only took a few minutes to reach her house, but she was very aware of Blake sitting beside her. At the scent of his shampoo, she leaned closer and inhaled deeply. His masculine presence had an unexpected effect on her, quickening her heartbeat a bit. She'd been attracted to him when he was younger, but he was a man now. A man who had been wounded in the war. There was an air of competence about him, of being able to handle whatever problem he faced. She felt calmer—safer—with him sitting beside her. He'd been quiet since they left the police station, and she kept stealing glances at him, wondering what he was thinking.

Carley batted back sudden tears. Nancy was *dead*. She'd never see her again, never talk to her, or share secrets. And she didn't know if she would ever get over that loss.

Her car was in the driveway and everything looked normal. No dark SUV hovered nearby. She closed her eyes and calmed her pounding heart, suddenly relieved that Blake was with her. Coming home alone after all that had happened would have been too hard.

She reached over and touched Blake's arm, feeling the corded muscles beneath his shirt. "Thanks for all you've done tonight. There's no doubt you saved my life."

He turned to face her. "I'm sorry I couldn't help Nancy. You two were still friends, I take it."

"Yes. Best friends." Her voice shook. "We even worked at the same place. I can't believe she's gone." Not wanting to talk any more, she started to get out but stilled when he placed his hand on her arm.

"I'll walk you to the door."

Carley started to protest, but suddenly she didn't want to be alone, standing out there in the night air, wondering if anyone was watching. She took a deep breath, grateful to Blake for being so protective.

He got out and strode along beside her, tall, broad-shouldered, calm, and competent. She felt protected just having him there. The night didn't seem so threatening with Blake by her side. When they reached the house, he held out his arm, blocking her way. She stared at him, wondering what was wrong.

He pointed to the front door and the fresh wood splinters around the doorknob. "Did your house look like that when you left?"

Carley stared at the damage, an icy shiver running through her. "No. No, it didn't."

Blake took hold of the doorknob and twisted gingerly, pushing it inward. Carley waited while he reached inside to turn on the light. From where she stood, she could see part of the destruction.

Someone had trashed her house.

Chapter Two

Carley stood transfixed, Blake's arm blocking her from entering her own house. The house someone had ripped apart. Sudden anger, blazing hot, flared through her. She knew he had his cell out and was talking with the police, but it was all she could do to keep from ordering him to get out of her way. She'd been chased and shot at, she'd lost her best friend, and now this. *God? Where are you? Why don't You do something? Don't You care anymore?*

She knew it wasn't God's fault, but she'd been through too much, too fast. A line from a poem that had comforted her in times past returned to her: sometimes when we don't realize He's even there, God will be carrying us. *Thank you, God, for being with me. I know You're always there. Don't let me forget it.* But seeing Nancy murdered and running in the dark through the park with someone shooting at *her* had been devastating. She'd had all she could handle.

Carley gave Blake a shove. "Get out of the way. I want to go inside."

He didn't even budge. Instead, he slid his arm around her, holding her back. "No, Carley. We can't go in. I know this is your house and you're upset, but it's also a crime scene. The police will be here soon, and we need to stay out until they come."

"What do you mean, a crime scene?" She craned her neck to see into her house. Tossed. Everything had been tossed.

"You know what I mean, Carley. We have to wait out here."

She knew he was making sense, and she appreciated the gentle concern in his expression, but that wasn't what she wanted. Blake Richards might have saved her life, but even if he still held her close against him, his touch warm and comforting, she wasn't about to let him tell her what to do.

Russ drove his black-and-white police car into the driveway. A fellow policeman with wavy black hair and a toned physique—Todd Walker—was with him.

Russ stopped at the foot of the step leading to the front stoop of the brick ranch-style house. "What's going on?"

Blake held Carley by the arm and moved her away from the door. She wanted to jerk loose, but he spoke before she could take charge. "Someone broke into

Carley's house and tore it apart."

The two men locked eyes and nodded their understanding of the situation. "Okay, let's take a look." Russ and Todd approached the house cautiously, as if even they were not certain of what awaited them inside. Blake ushered Carley through her own front door, still holding her arm so she had to stop just inside. Her mouth dropped open in shock as she looked at the destruction. This was a deliberate demolishing of her home. Who could have done such a thing—and why?

Russ stood for a minute, as if assessing the damage, then glanced at them. "We need to look around without you being in the way. Do you still have that screened-in porch?"

Carley nodded and watched as he walked through the living room to the sliding glass doors, avoiding the broken glass and scattered debris. He flipped on the outside light, stood for a moment looking, and flipped it off again. "All clear. You two wait out there while we go through the house."

Blake took her arm and steered her toward the door leading to the porch. Carley tightened her lips. She was getting tired of being ignored and led around by the arm. She was a grown woman and this was her house. Her *life*. And if they kept treating her like this, she was going to line them all up in about three seconds flat. And yes, she knew she was being unreasonable, but her nerves were still tied in knots. What she'd gone through tonight was enough to send anyone over the edge. Being shot at and grilled by the police weren't part of her usual routine.

The screened porch was dimly lit by the glow of the streetlight out front. Blake motioned toward the high-back wicker chairs. "We may as well get comfortable until they're through."

Carley didn't answer, just sank into one of the chairs and gripped the woven arms. What had happened to her quiet life? And what was she going to do about it? The damage to her home was bad enough, but Nancy was dead—brutally murdered—and the person who killed her had to be held accountable. A memory flashed across her mind of Nancy panicking, the gunshot, Nancy falling. Carley stiffened her shoulders in resolution and tightened her lips into a narrow line, her hands balled into fists. She was going to do all she could to help catch that man and make him pay in full.

Blake watched Carley, trying to guess what was going through her mind. Even sitting there looking mad enough to fight, her beauty shone. She'd been through a lot tonight, and on top of it all, the police were searching her house. This must have been the last straw, but his main concern was keeping her safe. Seeing her best friend murdered, running for her own life, and then finding out someone had broken into her house and tossed everything as if hunting for something—it was all too much to be coincidental. There wasn't any proof the killer and the person who broke in and trashed her house were the same, but he had a feeling the two events were connected.

"You have any place you can spend the rest of the night?"

She glared at him. "Yes, I have a place. Right here. This is my home, and I'm not leaving it."

He shook his head. "That may not be wise. Someone is obviously after you."

"And it may be connected to what happened to Nancy. I know that, but I'm not going to let them drive me out of my home."

"Carley, listen to reason. This guy may come back."

She hesitated and he could see she wanted to go with him, but then she tilted her chin and he knew what was coming. She had always been stubborn, even when she was wrong. "You don't understand. Nancy came to me for help, and I let her down. I've let too many people down. It's time to stand and fight."

She'd let too many people down? What did she mean by that? He didn't remember her being this concerned about anything except herself and what she wanted when they were in high school. Sure, he'd been attracted to her back then. Who wouldn't have been? With her blond hair and captivating blue eyes, always laughing, always having fun, going with the flow. She seemed different now, quieter, determined, but still stubborn. For the most part, people didn't change that much without a reason. Had something happened to change Carley from the carefree teenager to the defiant woman she was now?

She pulled her phone out and looked at it. From the way her body tensed, the rigid way she held herself, he had a feeling something was wrong. He edged closer, trying to get a look. Carley glanced up at him, eyes wide with shock. Blake reached over and took the phone from her. A text message leaped out at him.

GIVE ME WHAT I WANT AND I MAY LET YOU LIVE.

He stood and headed for the door, calling for Russ to join them in the sunroom. Russ read the message and nailed Carley with a stern look. "What do you have that he wants?"

She shook her head. "I don't know. I have no idea who this person is. How could I have anything that belonged to him?"

Russ cocked his head, eyes narrowed, eyebrows slanted, lips flattened into a tight line. "What he did to your house says different."

Carley glared at him, eyes spitting blue fire. "Listen to me! I have no idea what is going on here. My best friend was murdered in front of me. I was chased, shot at, and came home to a wrecked house. I'd be a fool to keep anything from you."

Russ didn't smile. "Hang on to that thought."

He turned and went back into the house, carrying her phone with him, and Carley turned to Blake, her blue eyes wide in disbelief. "He doesn't believe me. Why would he think I'd lie about something like this?"

Blake wasn't sure he believed her either. The Carley he'd known in school wouldn't have hesitated to be a shade less than truthful if it suited her. In fact, she'd lied about him to the girl he was dating. Told Amelia he didn't really care for her, that he was just trying to make Carley jealous. Not that there was any reason for that claim. There'd never been anything between the two of them, and she'd had no reason to be jealous. She'd caused problems for him more than once back then. Even though Blake would have liked to think Carley had moved past that behavior, he knew there could be another side. It was possible she and Nancy were mixed up in something a little more involved than the story she'd told the police.

But maybe she really was telling the truth. He had to consider that too. At any rate, someone did appear to be after her. The anger in her expression had faded, leaving her transparently vulnerable and frightened. Her hands were locked tightly in her lap. She sucked in her lower lip, features slack, and she seemed to fold tight into herself.

This was her parents' house. Where were they? He started to ask, but Russ appeared in the doorway again.

He handed Carley the phone. "We're through in here."

Carley looked at him. "Did you find anything to point to who did this?"

Russ shook his head. "Nothing. If you learn anything, call me."

Carley's expression tightened. "Always considering that I'm able to call. Maybe I'll get a bullet in the back the way Nancy did."

Russ looked at Carley. The grim set of his mouth and the hard stare he gave her irritated Blake. As much as she'd been through tonight, Russ needed to tone it down a little. "Let's hope it doesn't come to that. We're leaving now. We've done all we can, so feel free to put things back in order if you want to."

He left before she could say anything more, and Blake didn't blame him. Carley was getting her anger back. He was just glad it wasn't directed at him. He stood and held out his hand. "Come on. I'll help you. Where do you keep your trash bags?"

He felt a shock of awareness when their hands touched. From the look of surprise on her face, he wondered if she felt it too. Carley stared up at him, then turned and walked to the door. Blake followed, glancing around curiously. He'd just had time for a quick impression of the destruction while the police shepherded him and Carley out to the porch, but without Russ and Todd pushing them through, he saw the mess Carley was left with. Books had been jerked from the shelves, and couch and chair cushions hurled around the room. Broken glass and pottery shards from vases and figurines littered the floor.

Carley stared at the destruction, shoulders drooping, apparently shocked into silence. For one disturbing moment he wanted to pull her into his arms and tell her it would be all right. Then common sense kicked in. He had a hunch she'd had about all she could take, and he wasn't in a position to get involved with a woman. Any woman. Let alone one as beautiful and as unpredictable as Carley Sutherland.

Blake watched as she picked up a dented picture frame made of some kind of silvery metal holding a photograph of her parents. She stood looking at it, wearing such an expression of sorrow he almost lost his resolve to stay away from her. Why was he letting this woman get to him like this?

He had to break the silence. "Where are your parents?"

She batted her eyes as if coming out of a trance. Moving slowly, she walked toward the long, narrow mahogany table standing against the wall. She placed the frame on it and stood looking at the picture for a minute, bracing her hands on the tabletop as if for strength. Blake had about decided she wasn't going to answer when she spoke, her voice flat and devoid of emotion.

"They're dead."

His mouth dropped open. Dead? Both of them? Before he could say anything, she turned and walked into the other room, leaving him staring after her.

Carley sat, exhausted, at the kitchen table. The damage to things that were important to her—things that had belonged to her parents—had left her heartbroken. It had taken two full hours to restore the house to order. So many items were completely destroyed. Some of them weren't all that important, but there were others, things she'd treasured—like the Precious Moments figurines her mother had collected—that she was devastated to lose.

She'd never forget this night ... the worst night of her life. No, not the worst. She caught her breath, struck by the memory of a dark, foggy night; the shriek of crashing metal; her mother's scream. Carley had been driving. A truck had loomed out of the fog just as she started to turn onto a side road. In a matter of seconds, both of her parents were dead.

Carley swiped at the tears blurring her sight. She wouldn't cry, not with Blake in the next room. These were private tears, better shed in the confines of her bedroom, away from prying eyes and the condemnation of others. She'd experienced enough of that condemnation from those who blamed her for what had happened to her parents. And she had deserved every bit of it. If only she could go back and do that night over. But that wasn't possible. It was something she had to live with every waking moment of her life. That's why she didn't like to drive in dark, lonely places at night. She couldn't forget—couldn't forgive herself.

Blake stood in the doorway. "You okay?"

She nodded, too overcome with grief to speak. Her parents ... Nancy ... lost to her forever. She had no one left.

No, that wasn't true. She had the people at church who had made her welcome in the lonely months after her parents' death. People who had gone out of their way to be compassionate. Even the ones who had blamed her had, for the most part, come around to being friendly, if not exactly being friends. She had God. So why did she feel as if she had been completely forsaken? *Forgive me, Father. I know You're with me, and I'm sorry if I've acted like I think You don't care. It's just that I've been through too many things too fast tonight. I just can't get my head around it all.*

Blake pulled out a chair and sat, looking so concerned she almost broke down. She fought the impulse. If she started crying, she might never stop. She had to get control of herself. She could fall apart when she was alone. After all, over the years she had become fairly good at hiding her emotions.

His eyes caught and held hers. "Carley? You all right?"

"As right as I can be, I guess. It's been quite a night."

"It has at that. A lot to deal with. Are you sure you want to stay here alone? We've got an extra bedroom at the house. You're welcome to stay there."

She gave him a watery smile. "Stay in Mrs. Richards' house? She may have something to say about that."

He grinned. "She'd have a lot to say. All about how welcome you were, giving you advice, giving me orders. You were one of her favorite pupils."

Carley stared at him, stunned. "You have to be kidding. Me? You do remember what I was like in high school, don't you? I doubt if I was any teacher's favorite."

"Well, you were. She said you just needed a firm hand."

The smile faded from Carley's face. She *had* needed a firm hand, that was the truth, but her mother hadn't been much of a disciplinarian. If she had been, maybe Carley wouldn't have been so wild, and maybe Lillian Sutherland would still be alive.

Blake looked curious, as if he knew he'd said something that bothered her but had no idea what. She forced a smile. "Thanks for helping put the house back together. It was a real mess."

Even her bedroom had been searched. What could this jerk have been trying to find? Something connected to Nancy? But she had no idea what she was supposed to have that was so important. Everything had happened so fast it was all a confusing blur, a muddled mess in her mind. Maybe if she had time to pull herself together, without anything else happening, she could think more clearly.

Blake smiled. "No problem. What about my offer of a place to sleep? Mom would be happy to have you stay with us."

"I know. I see her at church and she's always extra nice to me. She teaches the older women's Sunday school class."

Carley pulled her attention away from him, away from the way he looked sitting at her kitchen table. He seemed relaxed, but she had a feeling he was alert, aware of every sound, ready to protect her if needed. He kept cocking his head, as if listening for something, and his slightly narrowed eyes glanced steadily around the room.

Blake's commanding presence had been absent in the all-American boy who had been good at all sports and had a job stocking shelves at Brennan's Grocery. Perhaps his time in the military had toughened some of Blake's softness. The change in him magnetized her, making it hard to look away. Back then, he had been a boy. Now, he was a man, in every sense of the word. Carley felt herself being drawn to him, just the way she had during high school. Whether she wanted them or not, those same feelings were creeping back, only stronger.

He grinned at her, his golden-brown eyes twinkling with sudden amusement. "Maybe I'll see you there on Sunday."

She hadn't seen him at Sunday worship services because she'd been filling in at the nursery, but her time of serving there was over. She'd probably see him this Sunday. And it pleased her—more than it should have.

Carley took a deep breath. It was time to end this. Time for him to leave. She made a show of glancing at her watch. "It's getting late. You'd better go."

Blake gave her a direct look. "I don't want to leave you here alone. Are you sure you won't come with me? I'll call Mom and tell her you're coming. She'll have your room ready by the time we get there."

It was tempting. Carley knew she'd be safe with Mrs. Richards, and she also knew she'd be safe with him. But she couldn't pull them into her problems. Yes, she was frightened, but she was too angry, too determined, to give up and run.

Carley realized she wasn't thinking all that clearly, but this was her home and she would stay here, trusting God to take care of her.

She shook her head. "I'll be all right. Whatever he wants, he must know by now that it's not here."

He looked at her for a long minute and then got to his feet, moving slowly, his worried expression revealing how reluctant he was to leave. "All right, if that's the way you want it. But if anything disturbs you, call Russ and then call me. I'm only two streets away, and I can be here before the police. And Carley, since you can't lock this door, do you have something you could wedge under it? That will usually block anyone from coming through."

Carley gave him a shaky smile, hoping he would leave before she burst into tears. She wasn't used to anyone watching out for her. "Yes. There are a couple of metal wedges out in the garage. And I'll call if I need you. I appreciate you, Blake, and all you've done for me tonight. Thank you."

He shook his head. "No thanks needed. I'm just glad I could be there for you."

Surely she was reading more into the light shining in his eyes and in the way he looked at her than he really meant. Could Blake Richards actually be interested in her? Carley rejected the very idea. No, he was just being nice because that was the kind of man he was. He would do as much for anyone who needed help. She walked him to the door and he hesitated.

"I'll see you tomorrow."

Tomorrow? He'd see her? The sudden warmth flashing through her at the thought surprised her. She pulled herself together enough to make her smile less glowing than she felt. "That will be good."

His hand reached out to touch her cheek. "Until tomorrow, then."

Carley swallowed a rush of tears as she watched him walk to his car. Blake was a good man. What would he think of her when he learned the way her parents had died? Would he be kind or would he be condemning? She didn't want to know. One thing she did know—there could be no future for her with Blake Richards. She wasn't his kind.

She glanced at the round wall clock with its elaborate black wire frame. Two o'clock in the morning? She stiffened as the silence closed around her. Nerves prickling, she looked at the shattered doorframe. Stay here? Was she crazy? Everything that happened tonight raced through her mind. She couldn't spend the night here alone.

Carley grabbed her purse off the couch. She should have gone with Blake, but it was too late. She'd spend the night at a motel, hoping the person who killed Nancy wouldn't see her car there.

Would she ever feel safe again?

Chapter Three

Carley woke, staring at the ceiling of the motel room, the previous night's events racing through her mind. She'd had a restless night, tossing and turning for a long time before finally surrendering to sleep. Sometime during the night, she had calmed down. She had also strengthened her resolve. Nancy had been her best friend, had stood by her all the way. Somehow she had to pull herself together and find out the truth about what had happened.

The last thing Carley wanted to do was go to work, but she'd probably be better off keeping to a normal routine than staying home, dwelling on Nancy's death and the assault on her own house. Besides, she couldn't learn anything by cowering at home.

Somehow she was going to get to the bottom of this. She owed it to her best friend to find the man who had killed her and, with God's help, Carley would do it, even if it cost her own life. After all, she didn't have that much left to live for.

She brushed aside the thought of Blake. He was a good, dependable man, and always had been. His mother raised him that way. But he had never been interested in her. No matter how hard she'd tried to entice him when they were in school, he'd avoided her, and he'd been gone for so long with college and the army, he probably had a woman waiting for him somewhere. A man as attractive as Blake wouldn't lack female companionship. He'd helped her and she appreciated it, but that didn't mean he wanted to be personally involved with her.

Carley dressed hurriedly and drove home to check out her house and get ready for work. She strode through the house, heartsick. The damage in the bedrooms and kitchen had been bad enough, but the living room would never be the same. The vases and figurines her mother had treasured had been shattered by the ruthless intruder. Surely there was no reason to destroy them other than a desire to frighten her. If so, he had definitely succeeded. But she wouldn't give in to fear. She couldn't.

She picked up the dented silver frame holding her parents' picture, almost reeling from the sudden wave of grief, shame, and guilt washing over her. They looked so young, so carefree. Her father's light hair was so much like hers, his slightly slanted smile barely hiding his laughter. Her mother's dark hair curled around her face, and her cheerful expression brought tears to Carley's eyes.

This was their home. They'd still be living here if she had been the daughter they'd deserved. Wiping tears, she set the picture down carefully on the mahogany table and snatched up her purse, too upset to eat breakfast. Just the thought of food turned her stomach. She hoped she could make it through the day without falling apart.

Carley stepped onto the front porch and pulled the door shut behind her, wishing she could lock it. Her neighbors on both sides and across the street would keep an eye on the house and call the police if they saw anything suspicious. This was a good neighborhood, and they looked out for each other. Despite that, Carley still wished more than her neighbors' watchful eyes roamed the street for the intruder.

A patrol car pulled into her drive and stopped. Russ got out and walked to the house. "Morning, Carley. How you doing?"

"Not all that great."

"I can understand that. You need to get new a new door installed today."

"I know. Apparently someone is after me." She tried to keep the sarcasm out of her voice. Of course, he already knew that, but she wasn't in a chatty mood this morning.

"Is there anything you can think of that might give us something to go on?"

"No, but I think it's rather obvious it's Nancy's killer. All of this started after she was murdered." She couldn't think of anyone else who would have this kind of grudge against her.

"You're probably right. Well, I'll get busy on it, see if I can find out anything. You may as well go on to work. I'll be in touch."

Carley didn't want to go to work. She wanted to lock herself in and hide from the person harassing her, but that would be playing right into his hands. She refused to become a captive of fear. Somehow, she had to learn who was doing this and what he wanted from her. "I want this person caught. If I'm not safe in my own house, where can I be safe?"

"We'll find out who's doing this, Carley. I promise you that."

She just hoped he solved this crime before she became the third victim.

Carley reluctantly got in her car and left, knowing at the end of the workday she'd have to come back and spent another restless night.

When she arrived at Quigley Enterprises, she barely had time to turn on her computer before she was summoned into her employer's office. Sherman Quigley—fairly tall, a bit overweight, gray hair receding from his forehead—motioned for her to take a chair. She sat down in the metal-framed chair across from his ancient oak desk, wondering what this was all about. A picture of a seashore graced one wall, and his desk was littered with pencils and scattered files.

He picked up a piece of paper, glanced at it, and laid it aside, his expression serious and intent, watching her. Which only amplified her last fragile nerves. "I suppose you know Nancy was killed last night."

"I know." Carley clamped her lips tight and gripped her hands together. It was all she could do not to burst into tears.

"You're her friend. Did she mention any problems she was having?"

Well, yeah. You could say that. Not that she'd had time to say much of anything. Mr. Quigley's eyes narrowed, strongly focused on her, the way her neighbor's cat would watch a mouse. The hair on the back of her neck prickled. What was this all about? His behavior seemed to be more than just a boss showing concern about an employee. It was more like he had a personal interest in what happened. Whatever he had in mind was making her extremely uncomfortable. She shook her head. "I can't imagine why something so terrible would happen."

Her best friend had found herself in a killer's crosshairs. That was the main problem she had. But judging from his stern expression and the way he kept staring at her, he had something definite in mind. Until she found out why the criminal had felt the need to murder Nancy and ransack her own home, until she learned what this conversation was about, Carley didn't intend to share anything further with Mr. Quigley. She didn't completely trust him. Occasionally she had noticed him doing things he wouldn't want others to know about. Not bad things, but enough to make her doubt him.

"Her work had been slipping for some time, and I was on the verge of speaking to her about it. I had the impression that she'd gotten mixed up with something she shouldn't be doing."

Carley shook her head again, denying what he was implying. "I never saw anything like that."

"I think it was there, just the same. She was a little confused at times. I suspected she was on drugs."

"Not Nancy. She wouldn't have anything to do with drugs. Her brother died of an overdose, and she hated anything to do with drugs and the people who sold them. Besides, if she had been taking something, I would have noticed. I can assure you that never happened."

"You can't really be sure. We all slip sometimes, and the people closest to us can be the last to know."

"If she had been upset for any length of time, I would have known. She told me everything. And it would have nothing to do with drugs. I'm positive of that."

He picked up a ballpoint pen and tapped it on the desk. "People can fool us. We tend to see what we want to, particularly if it concerns family members or close friends. If you learn anything about what caused this, I trust you will let me know. After all, she was my personal secretary, and I thought a lot of her."

Carley didn't believe a word he said. Why was he working so hard to convince her Nancy was into drugs? He was either trying to pump her for information, or he was trying to trick her into believing something that wasn't true. If Mr. Quigley had been the man Nancy had seen, she would have said so. Instead, she'd made it clear that she didn't know the man at the restaurant. That ruled out her employer, so why was he acting like this?

She filed the thought away to consider later, aware that Mr. Quigley was still watching her. Evidently, he wasn't finished. She waited, not speaking. He'd called the meeting—he could do the talking.

After a moment he shrugged. "That isn't why I called you in. I need someone to take Nancy's place. Her death has left me shorthanded. Would you be interested in working as my secretary? You've been here long enough to have absorbed the way business is handled, so you'd not require as much training as someone brought in from the outside."

Carley stared at him, not believing her ears. *Take Nancy's place?* Grief rocketed through her. He couldn't be serious—but he was waiting for her to answer. She cleared her throat, searching for the right words. "I"—she looked down and twisted her hands—"I don't think I'm qualified for something like that. I'm just a receptionist."

And she had no plans to change. The idea of taking Nancy's job made her sick, as if she would be trying to replace her best friend. She could never do that. She cringed just thinking about it. How could he be so unfeeling?

He gave her another considering look. "It wouldn't be all that hard. Juanita Osborn is Nancy's assistant. She'd be able to help you with anything you didn't know."

So why didn't he give the position to Juanita? "It seems to me she'd be the perfect person for the job. She's already trained. Why would you even consider asking me to take it on?"

He frowned. "She's old and will retire soon. I want to train someone who would be here long enough to do us some good."

Only God kept her voice low and calm. "That's not a decision I could make on the spur of the moment. I need time to pray about it."

He wasn't happy, but she didn't care. If he didn't like her answer, he could just get over it. She'd never given him much thought before. He was the boss, nothing more, nothing less. She had an unsettling feeling he couldn't be trusted. This was something she had to think about—not the job offer, but this new suspicion as to Mr. Quigley's motive for the opportunity and his apparent interest in Nancy's death. Something was going on, and until she learned what, she'd be on guard.

He finally let her go, but she was jittery, looking over her shoulder for the rest of the day. It was a relief when she could leave the plant. Being where she saw Nancy every day, facing memories everywhere she looked, plus Mr. Quigley's behavior, had stressed her nerves to the max. All she wanted was to get home and crash.

On her lunch break, she had called Joe Elliot's Construction to pick up a new door for her. She couldn't stay at her house the way it was. It took him three quarters of an hour to install the new door with a bright, shiny lock.

"That'll work, Carley," Joe said, "and I added a deadbolt and one on the back door too. But just the same, you hear any suspicious noise, you call the cops. Don't take any chances."

"All right, Joe. I appreciate all you've done." She paid him and he left, but his words kept ringing in her mind. *Call the police.* She definitely would. After what happened to Nancy, she wouldn't take any chances.

Her home phone rang, but when she answered no one was there. Dead air awaited her on the other end of the line, seemingly waiting for her to say something. "Hello?"

Silence.

She tried a couple more times, then hung up. Who was on the other end of that line? Could this be connected to Nancy?

Carley hurriedly pushed the thought aside. She was just upset because of what had happened. Not everything could be connected to Nancy's death.

The phone rang again and she hesitated before answering. Finally, she reached for the receiver to find Blake on the other end. "Hey, you doing okay?"

"I guess. Why? What's going on?"

"Nothing. I thought I'd drop by and I wanted to warn you not to cook. I'm bringing dinner."

Dinner with Blake? Carley hesitated. Was this a good idea? She had planned a quiet evening at home, unwinding after her stressful day, and Blake wanted to drop by and even bring something to eat? She decided to stop questioning Blake's motives for wanting to come by. It would be good to see him again, and at least she wouldn't be alone with her thoughts. His offer of dinner didn't necessarily mean anything; he was just being nice. And maybe having someone to talk to, just visit with, would help her relax.

"That sounds good. Thanks for thinking of it."

"Okay, see you in a few minutes."

Carley hurried to change into jeans and a deep rose sweatshirt. She ran her hands through her blond hair and applied a touch of lipstick. The doorbell rang before she got around to refreshing the rest of her makeup, but that was okay. It was just Blake and this wasn't a date. He was only being neighborly. Would he even notice the way she looked?

Blake glanced down at the basket he carried. It looked like he had enough food to feed four or five people. They would eat well.

Carly greeted him and led the way toward the kitchen. She helped him unpack the basket and their hands touched, sending an unexpected flash of warmth surging through him. Together they pulled out salad, hot rolls, his mother's famous chicken casserole—rich with the fragrance of stewed chicken and creamy sauce—green beans seasoned with bacon, and herbed potato wedges. Blake lifted an entire apple pie from the basket and breathed in the cinnamon fragrance.

"This is a feast. I'll have to call your mother and thank her."

"She'd be happy to talk to you. In fact, she was very put out because I didn't bring you home with me last night. She doesn't like you being here by yourself."

Carley smiled. "Really, I'm all right. Have you talked to Russ?"

Blake speared a potato wedge. "Yeah, but he didn't tell me anything I didn't already know. Anyway, I doubt they've learned much yet. Murders aren't usually cleared up that fast, and there wasn't much evidence left behind. He drove up and shot her, and while he did chase you, that didn't reveal anything about who he is. They're working on it, but it could take some time before they find out anything. And you have to realize they probably won't share anything they learn with us. This is a police investigation, and we're not a part of it."

Carley placed her fork on her plate as if she wasn't hungry. The thought of what had happened sort of dented his appetite too.

"I've thought he could be the one who wrecked my house, but how could he have known who I was? I'm sure he didn't get a good look at me. As soon as the shot exploded, I ran."

Blake hesitated and she cocked her head, giving him a stern look. He shrugged.

"I'm just guessing, but your car was there. There was probably something in the glove box—insurance cards or something—that gave him your name and address."

"Yes, of course. I hadn't thought of that."

She glanced around, looking for a way to change the subject. "You ready for pie? I have ice cream to go with it."

"That sounds good."

Blake watched as she bustled around the kitchen, getting out small plates for the pie and setting out the ice cream. Her figure was just as attractive as ever, and he couldn't keep his eyes off her. He wished things could be different, that they could just be two people who had met after a long separation, but that wasn't possible. He had a feeling Carley was in danger, and he was planning to do everything he could to take care of her.

Yes, Russ and the rest of the police force were working on it, but for some reason he couldn't walk away from her. Russ wouldn't like him getting involved, but Carley needed help and Blake didn't have anything else to do. No job, no responsibilities, just hanging around, waiting for military orders. He'd keep an eye on her, be around more than the police could.

She sliced the pie, served it, and sat down at the table. "I called Joe Elliot from work. He installed a new door and locks just before you called, so that should help."

"I noticed the door when I came in. I'm glad you got that taken care of. Are you comfortable with staying here alone?"

"Not comfortable, exactly, but I can handle it."

He stared at her, doubting she was as much at ease as she was letting on. They had to find out who was behind all this before the same guy got to Carley.

Chapter Four

Carley had taken off work to go to Nancy's funeral—the first one she had attended since her parents' death. Throughout the service she'd had a creepy feeling between her shoulder blades, as if someone was staring at her. She'd glanced around a few times, but no one seemed to be watching. After giving her regards to Nancy's family, she left the funeral home, relieved to be away from the reminders of everyone she had lost.

She approached the front of her house carefully, key in hand, and once certain nothing was different from before she left, she entered and searched her home.

Carley sat down in front of the television to eat her microwaved lunch—a frozen dinner from the grocery store. Probably she needed to cook more instead of living out of the frozen food department, but during times of stress, she preferred easy. She spent the rest of the day reading and checking her email, and even worked in an unintentional nap sitting in front of the computer.

Night was different. As the light faded outside, she grew more nervous. The silence of the house smothered her. She strained to hear every noise, reluctant to turn on the television because it might muffle the sound of someone trying to break in.

Finally, she went to bed only to lie there, nerves on edge. Night lights she'd placed in the living room and in the hall helped, but she stared at the open bedroom doorway anyway, unable to relax. Every time she dozed off, a car motor would roar on the street or the wind would lash branches against the house, jerking her awake. She could have gone back to the motel, but she had to get her life back to normal.

At least as much as possible.

The next morning, Carley woke groggy from lack of sleep after a restless night of tossing and turning before finally drifting off. She rubbed sleep from eyes and ran her hand through knotted hair, wishing she could stay home. She managed to push herself out of bed and head for the kitchen, dreading what the day might bring. The house was quiet—too quiet. Carley found herself listening for a door creaking, a footfall. She was alone, but still nervous. Would she ever feel safe again?

After a quick breakfast bowl of corn flakes, she showered, changed from her pajamas into black slacks and a blue button-down shirt, and went through the routine of makeup and combing her hair. The house was uncomfortably quiet. Suddenly she was in a hurry to leave, to be around other people, where she wasn't always straining to hear unexpected noises. She grabbed her keys and hurried out to her car.

Carley had only been at her desk for fifteen minutes when she glanced up to see Mr. Quigley looking down at her. "Have you made a decision?"

A decision about what? She had been so engrossed in the papers she was working on that it took a minute for her to register what he meant. "About the job?"

"Yes. I need to hire someone right away. Nancy's death left a hole I have to fill immediately. Work is piling up. Are you interested?"

Carley took a deep breath, wishing she could avoid this. "No, I don't think so. I've thought it over and I'd rather stay at the reception desk."

His expression hardened into granite. "Do you have any reason to turn down a top job like this? Most people would be thrilled to move up to a better-paying position."

"I'm sure there are others who would be happy to take the job. But not me. Nancy's death hit me hard. I was in the park with her when she was killed." The *Westfield Examiner* had published that nugget of story yesterday, so she might as well admit it. So much for trying to stay in the background. Not that it made any difference. The killer, if he was the one who broke into her house, already knew where she lived.

He raised an eyebrow. "I'd heard that. What were the two of you doing out there?"

"She called me to meet her. Someone was threatening her and she was scared. I'd just been there a few minutes when he drove up and shot her. I'm not over that yet. Taking her place would be too much for me at this time."

Mr. Quigley leaned against the desk, staring down at her in that intensely focused way he'd been using lately. "What did she tell you?"

"Not much. She didn't have time. Like I said, I'd just arrived at the park when he drove up. I'm lucky I managed to get away." She swallowed hard, trying to breathe normally. A lump filled her throat at having to say the words again. Telling the same story over and over was like a sword in her heart.

"She must have said something." His voice was flat, with no expression whatsoever, as if they were discussing the weather, but his eyes were piercing, nailing her with their directness.

"Just that someone tried to run her off the road and she was afraid to go home. Why?"

Let him answer that. And she wasn't going to tell him anything more. The rest of it was between her and the police. Besides, why was Mr. Quigley so interested? He had a reputation of avoiding small talk with employees, and he never encouraged idle gossip that only wasted time. Why was he spending time talking to her? He must have caught some hint of her mental questions because he made an obvious effort to relax his shoulders and stop staring at her so intently.

"Oh, I was just interested. After all, Nancy had been my personal assistant for three years now. I thought a lot of her, and this has upset me. Consider that job for a few more days. I think you'd be perfect for the position. Let me know if you change your mind."

He turned and walked toward his office, leaving her to stare after him. First, he had to fill the position immediately, but all of a sudden, he was willing to wait a few more days? That didn't add up. Why was he trying to talk her into taking that job? A chill crawled up her spine. She wanted to look away from him, but her eyes were drawn to that bulky figure with the cocky walk. He had something in mind, and she had a feeling it concerned her. Just how, she didn't know, but whatever it was, it didn't appear to be in her favor.

Blake parked in Carley's driveway at five thirty, waiting for her to come home. He wanted to follow up on something and wanted her to go with him. She pulled in beside him, rolled her window down, and smiled. "Blake. I didn't expect to see you. Is everything all right?"

"As far as I know. I had an idea. How would you like to drive out to The Old Mill for dinner? We can ask if anyone saw Nancy there or saw the man and woman she told you about."

Carley stared up at him, her lips pursed and a slight frown wrinkling her forehead. He realized she was thinking about it, not immediately accepting the invitation the way he wanted her to. Finally, she said, "That sounds like a good idea, but are you sure you want to get involved in this?"

He shook his head. "Don't even go there. I'm already involved. I got involved the minute I grabbed you in the park. We're in this together. Now, are you going with me, or do I have to go by myself?"

She shrugged. "I just got home. Can you give me a minute?"

"Sure. I'll wait out here."

He waited while she went inside. While she didn't seem excited about it, at least she was going. A few minutes later she hurried out the front door, locking it behind her. She had changed from the black pants and blue shirt she had worn to work into a dark pink blouse with gray pants and jacket.

Carley smiled and his heart kicked up a notch. "Sorry I kept you waiting."

"I didn't mind. We've got plenty of time."

They spent the drive to the restaurant talking about people they knew instead of speaking about the subject hovering at the back of their minds. It was good to just relax and talk, but Blake knew it couldn't last. Not when they were coming out to the restaurant to see what they could learn about the man Nancy had seen with Rachel Blevins, the woman who had been murdered and thrown away to lie in a ditch.

After the hostess seated them at a front table next to a window and handed them menus, Carley glanced around the restaurant. Antique kitchen items decorated the walls. Booths lined two sides and the rest of the room was filled with tables. An overweight man filled his plate at the salad bar that stretched across one end of the casual neighborhood restaurant. "I wonder where Nancy was sitting that night."

"I don't know, but maybe we can find out who was working then."

Blake motioned for the hostess to come back to their table. She approached them, eyebrows raised warily. After taking newspaper clippings from his wallet—one with a picture of Rachel Blevins, the second bearing a picture of Nancy—Blake placed them face up on the table. "Four nights ago, both of these women ate here. This one was with a man. Could you tell us who was working that night?"

She looked at the pictures, and Blake was sure color faded from her cheeks. After a moment she said, "I guess I was, but I didn't see anything."

"Anything? Do you mean you didn't see either of these women, or you didn't see anything happen?"

"Both." She stepped back away from the table. "And I wouldn't tell you if I had. I read the papers too. Both of those women are dead. I don't want anything to do with this."

Carley spoke up for the first time. "Don't you want to see their killer caught?"

The hostess shook her head. "Not if it means putting my life on the line. They're both dead. I can't do anything to help them now, and I have no idea who waited on them."

She whirled and strode away to assist a couple who had just entered. Carley huffed out a sigh and turned to Blake. "How can she be so unfeeling? Like she said, two women are dead. Why wouldn't she want to help?"

"She told you why. She's scared. Can you blame her? After all, she's not emotionally connected with either woman. You are. It's not the same for her."

He knew that wasn't what she wanted. She wanted the woman to give them a detailed description of the man who had been here, not be forced to listen to some commonsense discussion as to why the hostess wouldn't talk.

He waited, not saying anything, and finally she grimaced. "I guess so. But it's not what I wanted to hear."

"I know, but I doubt it will be that easy. If it was, the police would already have caught up with him."

Carley grudgingly agreed, but he knew she still wanted more. She wanted details, wanted facts. So did he, but it wasn't going to be that way. The waitress stopped at their table and they ordered, waiting until she left before bringing it up again. Carley stared out the window for a minute then turned to Blake. "I just remembered something. Nancy said she watched him put Rachel into a black SUV, then drive behind her car. I guess that's how he got the license number."

Blake nodded. "Probably, but I wonder how he knew Nancy was going to that meeting. She was about thirty miles from where she worked, so how would he know to follow her and try to run her off the road?"

Carly sighed and shook her head. "It seems like everything we come up with just opens up more questions."

A few tables over, a man stared at them, not even bothering to look away when Blake glanced in his direction. Phil Peterson. He recognized him although he hadn't seen him for several years. His light brown hair was longer than he remembered, but those cold gray eyes were the same. He'd had a crush on Nancy, even dated her a few times, but it hadn't turned out well. He'd been too overbearing, not wanting her to see her friends, just him. The way Blake had heard it, Carley had successfully urged Nancy to break it off with him, and he hadn't taken it lightly.

Blake noticed her glancing at Phil and then looking away, seemingly disturbed by the way he was staring at her, his expression hard, eyes cold and calculating. When Blake glanced back later Phil was gone, but Carley's flushed cheeks and crinkled brow belied her steady voice. She was upset.

While driving home, Blake thought about their evening out. They hadn't learned anything helpful, and except for the encounter with Phil, it had been a good evening, just the two of them sitting and talking. He'd like to do more of that. Something not related to the mystery—just be together, a man and woman interested in each other. Looking at her now, his pulse beat a little faster. She was a beautiful woman, but there was more to her than that. She was a fighter, not giving up although she certainly had reasons enough to be afraid, but there was also a softer side to her, and he wanted to do something to bring it out more often. But she hadn't shown much interest in developing a relationship. Perhaps he could do something to change that too.

A blue Dodge had been behind them since they drove out of The Old Mill's parking lot. Was someone following them, or was he being overly cautious?

"What kind of car did you say the guy who shot Nancy drove?"

Carley jerked around to face him. "A black SUV. Why?"

"Just curious." He didn't know anyone who drove a vehicle like the one behind them, but that didn't necessarily mean the driver of the Dodge was Nancy's murderer. He had no idea what most people drove. Seldom paid attention. A car fanatic he was not. He sped up. The car behind them did the same. Blake slowed down. The Dodge slowed too. He was just getting ready to reach for his phone and call Russ when the car turned off onto a different road and disappeared from sight.

Maybe his nerves were getting the best of him. They hadn't told anyone they would be at the restaurant, so no one would be following them—unless it had been Phil.

Blake glanced over at Carley. She'd been quiet since they left the restaurant.

Probably upset because they hadn't learned anything. Well, he wished they'd learned more too, but life didn't always work the way they wanted. "I've been away so much, I've forgotten a lot. Where did Nancy live?"

"Over on the north side of town in her parents' house. They moved to Arizona to be closer to Willadean, Nancy's older sister. She's lost her husband, and she has cancer. They went to take care of her and her children, and Nancy stayed here."

As he drove them to the Wilkins' address, the house owned by Nancy's parents, he thought again how good it was to have Carley sitting beside him. He was beginning to develop feelings that went a lot further than friendship or just attraction. Feelings that were becoming more difficult to keep under control. It was getting harder to hide how he felt. So maybe he needed to start showing a little more attraction, let her know he wasn't just interested in being friends. The way he felt about her was much stronger than friendship. Of course, he had something else to consider. He couldn't only focus on building a relationship. He also had to come up with a way to keep her safe.

Carley pointed toward a pale green one-story house set on a fairly large lot. A white Buick sat in the driveway. "That's her house."

Blake slowed down, looking it over. He braked, checking out the front door. Was it his imagination, or was it slightly open? He backed up and then turned into the driveway. Carley looked at him, a question in her eyes. He fumbled for his cell phone. "Maybe I'm off base here, but it looks to me like someone has been inside. I'm calling Russ to take a look."

Carley whipped around to stare at the house. "You're right. The door isn't closed all the way."

"We'll wait here until he comes."

Ten minutes later, Russ drove up and parked behind them. "All right, let's see what's going on."

He strode toward the house and they followed. The door was splintered, just the way Carley's had been. Russ pushed the door open and looked inside. Blake, standing behind him, could see the same type of damage that had been done to Carley's house. Someone had trashed it.

Russ, now furious, ordered them to go sit in the car, then he called for a team to come help him sort through the mess. An hour later, the men came out and closed the door. Russ walked over to Blake's car to talk to them. "So you just happened to be driving by and noticed the door wasn't shut? You sure you weren't inside?"

Blake shook his head. "I told you we just saw it."

Carley glared at him. "We didn't even get out of the car. Why don't you get over suspecting me and look for the person doing this? Do you actually think I would hurt Nancy?"

Something flickered in his eyes. Compassion? Regret? Whatever the emotion was, it vanished almost immediately. He turned away to watch one of the police cars leaving the drive. "Her house is a mess. They really trashed it. I'll have a new door put up and get a cleaning service to take care of it."

"No," Carley objected. "I'll clean it. I can do that much for Nancy."

Russ looked like he wanted to argue, but then after a minute, his shoulders dropped. "All right, but you'll need help."

"I'll help," Blake said. "If we find anything out of order, we'll call you."

After a pause, Russ nodded. "I don't think you'll find anything. We looked through it pretty good. But if you do, I want to know."

He left, and Blake and Carley resumed their trip back to her house. "It's too late to do anything this evening. We'll start on it on Saturday. And I think you need to call John Austin and get an alarm installed. That may stop this jerk from bothering you again."

She looked like she might rebel, but then she nodded. "That may be a good idea."

Once back at Carley's place, he walked through the rooms, making sure everything was all right. The master bedroom was overly neat and clean, as if it wasn't used all that much. On the other hand, the bedroom he assumed was Carley's showed signs of being used. A small basket holding a potted ivy sat on one side of the dresser. A light blue robe was draped over the back of a comfortable chair and a pair of scuffed tennis shoes lay beside the bed. He liked visualizing Carley here. Not just in this room, but throughout the house, stirring up something delicious in the kitchen, relaxing in the living room. He felt a growing desire to share that life with her. He hated to leave her here alone, but she was too stubborn to listen to reason.

All he could do was drive by occasionally and pray that God would keep her safe.

Chapter Five

The phone was ringing when she opened her front door after work. Carley answered to find Blake on the line. "Hey, how about going out to dinner? There's a new restaurant in town I thought we could check out. And I've got something we need to talk about."

Carley smiled at the enthusiasm in his voice. Eating out twice in one week? After the way she had chased him in high school with no results, having him call her for a date was a treat. But was it a date? Maybe he just wanted to talk about all that had happened. She made up her mind abruptly. Whatever the reason, she wanted to see him, wanted to sit across the table from him—just be with him.

"That sounds great. What time?"

"Oh, I'll give you thirty minutes? That long enough?"

"I'll make it work." She hung up the receiver and hit her bedroom. Thirty minutes? Did the man have any idea how long it took a woman to get ready to go somewhere? By the time he rang the doorbell, she was ready and waiting, but she had probably broken the all-time female record for changing clothes and redoing her makeup. She deserved a medal.

The Traveler served food she'd never heard of from several different countries—colorful and spicy seafood paella from Spain; salty, fried fish and chips from Great Britain; and almond-and-rose-flavored marzipan from Germany. All of it sounded delicious. She needed to get out more to find out what was going on in town.

Blake grinned at her. "Decided what you want?"

"A bit of everything, but I'm leaning toward the chicken piccata." At least she knew what it was. Chicken browned in butter and seasoned with fresh lemon and capers.

"That sounds good. I'll have that too."

The waitress took their orders and left. Blake leaned back in his chair. "So how did it go today? Anything new happen?"

Carley breathed in the delicious fragrances wafting through the restaurant. She considered telling him about Mr. Quigley but decided not to. Her boss's behavior couldn't have anything to do with the case, and it might be a good idea to let what happened at work stay there. At least until she learned otherwise. "Nothing. How about you?"

"No, but I'm wondering how the killer knew Nancy was in the park. You said she called you. That right?"

"Yes. And I don't like driving outside of the main area of town at night, but she sounded so upset I had to go."

"Okay, he couldn't have been following her, because you got there before he did."

Carley stared at him, chilled. "Do you think he followed me? But how could he have known where I was going?"

"That's the question, and no, I don't think he was following you. I don't know what I think, actually. There's not that much to get hold of."

Carley had been feeling uncomfortable for several minutes. Nothing she could put her finger on, just that same itch between her shoulder blades, a sense of being watched. She glanced around the room, but no one seemed to be paying any attention to her. A tall man, broadly built like a football player, with short, clipped black hair and a goatee was sitting at a table across the room from them. The woman with him was talking, head tilted, chin lifted a notch. Her long brown hair fell past her shoulders, and her raised eyebrows and overly alert expression shouted how important she was.

The man wasn't really handsome—eyebrows a little too bushy and his jaw line prominent—but there was something about him that caught the eye. Carley noticed the way the waitress was actually flirting with him while the woman Carley assumed was his wife was sitting right there. He wasn't doing anything to encourage her, but he wasn't rebuffing her either. The wife's lips tightened, thinning to a fine line.

Curious, Carley glanced at Blake. "That couple over there. Do you know them?"

Blake looked in their direction, then back at Carley. "Yeah, I know them. She's Marlene Lister. Her father, Grover Barnes, was a state senator. He started Barnes Manufacturing over in Oldham. She runs it now. The guy is her husband, Kurt Lister. Why?"

"No reason. They just caught my eye. She seems to be doing all the talking."

Blake laughed. "Well, she's that way. Marlene thinks a lot of Marlene. Kurt was a salesman at the plant until they got married. Now he works with her in management, but I've heard she holds the reins with a tight hand. I've always wondered what it would be like, taking orders from your wife."

"Depends on the wife, I suppose, but just looking at him, I'd guess he wouldn't enjoy it." Carley searched for a way to change the subject. This was too much like gossip, and she was sorry she had brought it up.

The Listers, one of the town's most prominent and well-known couples, stopped by their table on their way out. Kurt didn't say much, but he kept watching Carley. Something in the appraising way he looked her up and down sent chills down her spine. Carley mentally shook off the goosebumps and glanced at Blake, immediately soothed by his calm demeanor. She had enough problems. Kurt Lister was one she didn't need.

Marlene looked at Carley. "Are you the woman who was in the park with that Nancy who got killed?"

That Nancy? Carley stiffened her spine. "Yes, I was there."

She resented the question. Maybe it was the way this woman was looking at her, with eyebrows raised, as if she was a cut above everyone else. People like that really irritated her. Although she knew it was wrong to feel that way, she longed to take Mrs. Self-Important Lister down a notch.

Marlene's lips drew back in what could pass for a smile if you weren't too particular. "That must have been dreadfully frightening."

Carley shrugged. "Just in the wrong place at the wrong time."

She wasn't about to unburden herself to this woman or reveal how devastated she was by Nancy's death.

The man stared down at her. "Do you have any idea who did the shooting?"

"No. If I did, I'd tell the police. I'd like to see him pay for what he did. No one deserves to be killed that way."

It was his turn to shrug. "Most people have a reason for what they do."

"No one has a right to kill someone else. The person who murdered Nancy needs to be punished."

"An eye for an eye and a tooth for a tooth?" He smirked.

Carley took a deep breath, totally resenting him quoting the Bible, as if she were in the wrong for believing the killer should be brought to justice. "Our actions have consequences. Whoever this person is, when he killed Nancy, he placed himself outside of the protection of the law."

Marlene gave that tight smile again. "Well, it's been nice meeting you, but we need to be going." She grasped her husband's arm and he nodded at Blake, ignoring Carley as they turned and walked away.

Carley took a deep breath and glanced across the table at Blake. "Sorry. I didn't intend to be rude, but all those insinuations about right and wrong for a murder bothered me. I didn't handle it very well."

Blake grinned. "Actually, I believe you handled it very well indeed. I couldn't have done it better myself. And no apology needed. The Listers aren't my kind of people either. They seem to think the rest of us exist to serve them. Forget it. They're not worth getting upset over."

Carley rearranged the silverware, not looking at him. Nancy's death was too brutal and the memory too strong. She still wasn't handling it well. "I know, but my temper got the best of me. I think of Nancy and get angry all over again." She chanced looking at him since her blood pressure had dropped after the Listers walked away. "Are we still putting her house back in order tomorrow?"

Anger. One of the things she had trouble controlling. She never used to be this way—until her parents died. Since then, she could get irritated at the slightest thing. She'd asked God to help her, but so far nothing seemed to be working.

"That's the plan. I'll pick you up around nine."

Blake watched Carley, knowing she was still upset. Cleaning up the mess at Nancy's would be hard on her. He would suggest she stay home and let him do it, but he knew he'd be wasting his breath. One thing about Carley Sutherland—she was a tough lady. A lot of people would have broken under all she'd gone through lately. She just became stronger and more determined.

She nodded with her head tilted a little to the left, looking down, her eyes listless. "Nine will be all right. Poor Nancy. She didn't deserve this."

"No one deserves to die by violence," Blake said, remembering friends he'd seen die in battle, young lives cut off too early—families left to grieve. That was war, and the brave men and women he'd served with had volunteered for the job, but Nancy hadn't volunteered for anything. She'd been an innocent bystander, a witness to the action preceding a murder. Now she was dead too. He shook his head at the unfairness of it all.

The restaurant door opened and Russ entered. Blake glanced at Carley to see if she'd noticed. The policeman stopped by their table, his expression bland, neither friendly nor unfriendly. "Well, this is a coincidence. I've been meaning to have a talk with the two of you."

"Oh?" Blake tilted his head to look up. "What about?"

"Just wondering if you had remembered anything new. Anything happen that I don't know about?" This last was addressed to Carley.

She shook her head. "Not really, but I've had a creepy feeling a few times, like someone is watching me."

"I can't act on a feeling, but if you see anything suspicious, call me immediately. I don't care how minor it is—call."

Blake noticed Carley looked a little more relaxed at Russ's words. He knew she was nervous, and she had a reason to be. So far, they had no idea who was behind this wave of crime directed at her.

Russ changed the subject. "I hear the two of you were out at The Old Mill asking questions. You trying to do our job for us? You need to stay out of the way and let the police do the investigating."

Carley got that stubborn expression again, and Blake knew what was coming. No way would she do what Russ was suggesting. She was too bullheaded for her own good, and he couldn't do anything about that. What he could do was be there, help her, and protect her when he could.

She frowned at Russ. "I can't do that. I owe it to Nancy to do everything I can to find her killer. She'd do the same for me."

"And get yourself killed in the process."

"I may get killed anyway. I was there. He can't be sure I didn't see something that would point to him. He probably thinks I'm a threat as long as I'm alive."

Blake knew that was the truth, but he didn't like hearing it said out loud that way. He was starting to realize how much Carley was beginning to mean to him.

Russ glanced at him. "Can't you make her see what she's doing is dangerous?"

As if she didn't know that. Blake gave him back look for look. "No, I guess I can't, so it looks like I'll have to help her. By the way, you might have a talk with the hostess there. I got the feeling she knew more than she would tell."

Russ shot Blake a stern look. "I'll keep that in mind. But as for your behavior, I can't stop you, but you interfere in my investigation and I'll arrest you."

"That's okay. At least we know where we stand."

"That's right, we do." Russ walked to a distant table and ordered without even looking at a menu. Carley looked at Blake, and the way her eyes shone struck to the heart of him. "Do you mean that?"

"Every word of it. I'm with you all the way. I don't know if we can find out anything or not, but we'll give it our best shot."

"Thank you for saying that, but I don't want you to get hurt."

"I don't want you to get hurt either, and we're going to do everything we can to take care of each other."

Something tugged at Blake's heart. An emotion he'd never experienced before. He'd dated other women, of course, had even been fond of a couple of them, but none had caught his heart the way Carley did. He wasn't sure what to call it, but he did know he'd do everything in his power to keep Carley safe. *Help me, Lord. I can't mess this up. Too much depends on it.*

Carley had all of the physical beauty of their high school days—actually, she was even more beautiful—but there was a difference in her, a strength, a sweetness she'd not had back then. He'd seen her at church. Had Carley found God? That would account for the change in her, and he hoped it was true. He had a feeling they wouldn't make it through this task they'd set for themselves without God's help.

She squeezed his hand. "You can count on that. You said you wanted to talk about something. Did it have to do with this?"

"As a matter of fact, it did. I'm making a list of people to talk to. I want you to look at it and see if you have someone to add. Anyone who might have known Rachel or seen her with someone."

"All right. Do you have it with you?"

He pulled a folded sheet of paper out of his pocket and handed it to her. She unfolded it and read through the list. "I see you have a check mark by some names. Have you talked to them?"

"Yes, and only one guy had something to tell me. He'd seen a black SUV in her driveway a couple of times, but he didn't get a look at the driver. The rest hadn't seen anything. How about you talking to the people you work with—was there anyone Nancy was close to? Someone she knew well enough to tell about what she saw? Maybe show them the picture before she left for that meeting?"

"I don't know for sure, but I'd say not. Nancy talked a lot, but there were certain things she kept quiet about. This seems to be one she would have kept to herself."

"But you can ask?"

"Yes, I can do that. Anything else?"

"I don't know. It's just that there must be someone out there who saw Rachel and him together. It doesn't seem possible they could have dated and no one knows anything about it."

"There's the wife too, if he was married," Carley pointed out. "I'd think she'd be suspicious if he was gone from home at night very often."

"Yeah. We don't know whether he was married or not, or who she may be, but it's an angle." He wasn't sure they would succeed, but he felt like they had to try.

Carley looked serious. "Are we going to do this behind Russ' back? He won't be happy if we mess up his investigation."

"We're not going to mess up anything. We'll just talk to people, take notes on what they have to say, and if we learn anything, we'll tell him."

She looked like she wasn't sure about all of this, but then her expression changed, determination crossing her face. "I'll do everything to find this coward. Whatever you decide to do, I'm in."

"Coward?"

"What else could he be? Shooting women? They were unarmed, with no way to fight back or defend themselves. He can't be much of a man to do that."

He couldn't argue with her on that point.

Blake took her arm after they finished their meal and he paid the bill, holding her close against his side as they walked to his car. All of his senses were alert as they strode across the parking lot. Surely no one would attack them here in front of the restaurant, but he still hurried Carley through the brightly lit area to the relative safety of the car.

The trip to her house only took a few minutes, and he parked in the driveway, knowing the moment had come to tell her goodbye and walk away. It was harder to leave her every time. He needed to get himself under control. Soon he'd be going back overseas. He'd seen a couple of friends get letters from the women they loved, claiming they couldn't handle the long separation and they'd found someone else. He'd witnessed the devastation the men went through. Falling in love with Carley could lead to him being in the same situation. Blake wasn't sure he could handle it. But she grew more important to him every day. He had to do all he could to keep her safe, even if the close contact fed the growing attraction between them.

Carley unlocked her door and turned to face him. Acting on impulse, he slid his arms around her, pulling her close. She stared up at him, her eyes shining like stars. Maybe she was starting to fall for him just as he was for her. Blake drew her closer, bending his head to press his lips to hers. A warm shock, like electricity, shot through him. He drew back to look at her. Her parted lips and the dazed look in her eyes showed she had felt it too.

He kissed her again, gently this time, but the warmth was still there. "Carley…"

She shook her head. "I know, Blake, but I can't go with you. I have to get on with my life, learn to live here again without fear. I can't do that if I run away. I'll be all right. God will take care of me."

He believed. Of course he did. But this guy had killed two women. What could stop him from going after a third?

Chapter Six

Blake picked Carley up at nine, and they drove the short distance to Nancy's house in comparative silence. Their kiss last night ... the way she had felt in his arms ... just thinking about it sent a surge of electricity rushing through him. She was so beautiful, so fascinating. He'd never known a woman like her.

Russ was parked in the driveway, waiting for them.

"What's he doing here?" Carley grumbled. "This will be hard enough without him breathing down our necks."

"I suspect he'll tell us as soon as we get out," Blake said, his voice calm and meant to be reassuring. Knowing Carley, it probably didn't work.

"Humph!" Carley slumped back against the seat, evidently not willing to cut Russ any slack.

Russ approached and unlocked the new door before handing the key over. Blake had a hunch that only ratcheted her irritation up another notch. "It's pretty much a mess, and we didn't help by looking through it. If you find anything that even might pertain to the case, you call me immediately. Don't try to decide if it's important. Let me make that decision."

Blake promised and Russ left. Carley twisted her lips and shrugged, as if dismissing Russ. "He's upset."

"He's just afraid we'll get in his way or mess up the evidence. He thought a lot of Nancy."

Carley looked thoughtful, as if she was struck by his words. Nancy and Russ used to be an item, but that was over long ago. Or was it? Blake didn't know, but if Nancy and Russ had started dating again, it would explain the policeman's disagreeable behavior toward Carley.

"Are you ready to get started? This is going to take a while."

Inside, Carley's mouth dropped open and her eyes widened as she stared at the way Nancy's home had been destroyed. The damage here was even worse than it had been at her house. A brass candleholder had been used to break the mirror over the fireplace mantle, shattering the glass and denting the holder's bottom rim.

Hidden Danger

The glass in picture frames had been smashed, books ripped apart, and even the shelves in the refrigerator jerked out, the contents spilled on the floor.

Carley entered the guest bedroom and started restoring order. Blake had a feeling she thought there would be fewer personal items in there and it would therefore be less painful to handle things that had once belonged to her friend.

A couple of hours passed as they sorted carefully through the mess, separating what could be saved from what had to be thrown away. Every item had to be handled and inspected for damage. As Blake worked in the kitchen, something suspicious caught his attention.

"Hey, Carley! Could you come out here?" He stood in front of a corner cabinet holding a plastic bag. Carley squinted at it. "What's that?"

"If I'm not mistaken, it's cocaine. I found it in the cookie jar."

"Cocaine!" Carley swung around to look at him straight on. "That's not Nancy's! She would never have had anything to do with drugs. I know her better than that. Someone had to have put that there to make it look like she was involved with it."

"It's in her house."

"I don't care if it is. She wouldn't have anything like that in her house."

"Maybe she was dealing."

Carley took a deep breath. "Be quiet and listen. I am telling you that whatever that is, it never belonged to Nancy. That's evidence of some sort, but it has nothing to do with her. Someone else put that there to make it look like she was into drugs."

"Someone also killed her."

"That's right, but not over drugs. Now you call Russ and tell him what you've found, or I will."

"I wasn't blaming Nancy..."

"Well, it sounded like you were. Call Russ. As if it's not enough that Nancy's dead and her house has been trashed, now someone is trying to destroy her reputation."

Blake held up his hand in surrender. "I give up. As soon as I call Russ, it's out of my control. He's in charge. He can take care of it."

"So make the call," Carley demanded, looking like she was determined to stand there and wait until he did. Like she wanted to hear every word he said to Russ.

Blake frowned at her, but he pulled out his cell phone and started dialing. He stuck to the basic facts, not putting blame on anyone, then hung up. "Satisfied? He'll be here in a few minutes. You can tell him what you think. I'm out of it. But if you're so sure she wasn't involved with drugs, what got her killed?"

Carley shot him an exasperated scowl. "I told you what, but you won't listen. She saw the face of a killer and he got rid of her. Now he's out to discredit her so no one will believe anything good about her. Nancy was innocent of everything except seeing the man with Rachel Blevins right before she was murdered. That's what sent him after her."

Blake stared at her, realizing he either had to believe her or walk away. And he would not walk away. He couldn't. He was in this to the end. "So, saying you're right, what are we going to do about it?"

Carley faced him, hands on her hips. "We're going to find out who killed her. What did you think we were going to do?"

He looked at her, with her blond hair gleaming like spun gold and blue eyes flashing fire, and thanked God for bringing this woman into his life. "That's what I thought we were going to do. Now we have to make plans about how and where to start."

Someone pounded on the door and Carley hurried to let Russ in. He entered the kitchen frowning, with his fists clenched and eyes narrowed. "What's this all about?"

Blake handed him the bag and pointed to the ceramic cookie jar shaped like a giant cupcake. "It was in there."

Russ opened the bag and sniffed the contents, eyes on Carley. "It wasn't there when we searched the house. We'd have found it. Someone had to have put it there after we left."

Carley stepped in front of him, red spots burning in her cheeks. Blake stretched out a hand, intending to stop her, but he was too late.

"We didn't put it there, if that's what you are thinking. And I'm sorry I lived and Nancy didn't, but that doesn't give you a reason to treat me like this."

Blake opened his mouth to say something, but Carley waved off his response. She stared at Russ as if daring him to disagree with her, but he blinked first.

His expression crumpled. "Nancy and me ... we were getting back together. She probably didn't tell you because she didn't fully trust me. We broke up before because I cheated on her."

Carley nodded. "Patrice Rosten."

Russ nodded, looking shamefaced. "I was a fool. God was giving me another chance, but now she's dead and what we were trying to rebuild is over. It was my job to drive out there and find her." He stared at Carley. "And it hurt that she turned to you instead of me. I may have been able to keep her safe."

"I've thought of that. She would have told you. She just didn't make it that far. The two of us have depended on each other for so long, it was second nature for her to call me. That doesn't mean she loved me more than she loved you. She was so scared she wasn't thinking straight."

"But you got to tell her goodbye. You got to talk to her."

"No, Russ, I didn't. There wasn't time for that. She'd just started to tell me what was wrong when he drove up. It's like he murdered her so she couldn't tell anyone about him."

Blake watched as Russ took all this in. He could only imagine how he would feel if something like this happened to Carley. Probably he wouldn't have kept his head as well as Russ had. He had to cut the guy a break. "So what are we going to do?"

Russ straightened. "There's no *we*. This is a job for the police. You two stay out of it."

Blake shook his head. "As long as this guy is running loose, Carley isn't safe. You can't expect me to just get out of the way and wait for him to find her. You wouldn't have done that to Nancy. And I'm not going to abandon Carley."

Russ glared at him, not saying anything.

Blake gave him back look for look. "I'll not get in your way, but I'm going to do everything I can to keep Carley safe."

After a moment, Russ nodded. "All right. But don't interfere in my investigation. I want this guy too bad to let him get away because amateurs messed up."

"Fair enough," Blake conceded. "I'm not trying to cause trouble. I just have an interest in this too."

"I understand that. And I think we understand each other now."

Carley watched them, totally irritated. Just a couple of good old boys making decisions for the little woman. And yes, she may be out of line even thinking this way, but she'd about had enough. Ever since Nancy was shot she had been pushed aside while the men took control. Well, she had a part in this too, and if they thought they could leave her out, they had another thing coming. Blake Richards might as well learn, and the sooner the better, that she was no delicate flower of a female. She was involved in this hunt for a killer, and she could pull her weight as well as any man.

They went back to cleaning after Russ left, and an hour later the house was as neat as they could make it considering everything that had been destroyed.

Blake moved a chair into a better position and looked at Carley. "You ready to leave?"

"I guess so."

A knock on the door interrupted the conversation. Blake strode across the living room to find Mr. Quigley standing on Nancy's front stoop. "I hope I'm not interrupting anything."

"No, of course not," Blake assured him. "What can I help you with?"

Mr. Quigley peered past him to Carley. "Oh, there you are. I was wondering if you've found Nancy's appointment book. I want someone to follow up with what she was working on, so I need that book."

"What did it look like?"

He held his hands up about a foot apart. "It was about this size, black, vinyl cover. She carried it with her all the time."

Questions raced through Carley's head. She'd been with Nancy a lot, at work and in their personal lives, and she didn't remember seeing anything like that. Surely if she'd had an appointment book and kept it with her, it would have shown up once in a while.

"No, we haven't seen it, but wouldn't she keep a list of her appointments in her computer? Seems to me she would."

"No, I've looked, but there's nothing there. Are you sure you haven't seen it?"

Carley watched Blake shake his head at Mr. Quigley's question. "No, nothing like that showed up here."

"I see. Well, did you find anything interesting?"

The tone of his voice had changed subtly, and Carley straightened, looking more alert. "No, nothing interesting. Just cleaning up the mess some jerk made. The guy really trashed the house. I hope the police catch him. He needs to pay for all he's done."

"Yes … I suppose so." Mr. Quigley stepped back from the door. "Well, I'll run along, don't want to bother you anymore."

Carley stood beside Blake, so close she could feel the warmth as his arm brushed against hers. She stared at her boss' back as he retreated down the walk, dressed in a suit as if he'd just come from work. What could Nancy have that could be that important? "I wonder what he really wanted."

Blake slid his arm around her waist and drew her away from the door, closing it. "I don't know, but something didn't seem right. What's he been like at work?"

Carley thought about it and decided to tell the truth. "He wants me to take Nancy's job." Her voice quivered with outrage at the thought. "Do you think he knew about the drugs in the cookie jar?"

"You mean he might have been the one to put that bag there?" Blake's arm tightened, pulling her around to face him. "You listen to me. If that guy or anyone else does anything that upsets you or makes you uncomfortable, you tell me and I'll take care of it."

Their eyes met and a warm little quiver raced up Carley's spine. She forgot her outrage at the big, brave men taking care of the poor, helpless little woman. All she could think about was the warm glow in his eyes and the way his lips turned up at the corners. She'd never had anyone who looked at her that way or promised to take care of her.

He smiled down at her, as if he understood how she felt. "I mean it, Carley. I'm here for you, whatever happens. I'll not let anyone hurt you."

Although she knew he couldn't be with her all the time, she realized Blake meant everything he said. *Thank You, God, but You take care of him. Please don't let him get hurt trying to help me.*

Because the man who was after her didn't seem likely to let anyone or anything get in his way to stop him—and that included Blake Richards.

Chapter Seven

Carley put in a full day at work while trying to avoid Mr. Quigley. Complete avoidance wasn't possible, but to her relief, he didn't mention Nancy or the secretary job. In fact, he ignored her. She stayed at her desk, avoiding the break room, and went to lunch alone, all too aware of the curious glances from her fellow workers. After work, too tired to think about fixing anything to eat, she drove to Peggy's Home Cooking.

Everyone in town must have had the same urge—the place was packed. Peggy had added a touch of country comfort décor to go along with the name of the restaurant. Ceramic chickens of all colors and types filled high shelves along the wall. Paintings of waterfalls, flower-covered hills, and colorful trees graced the wall. The employees all wore jeans and dark blue tee shirts bearing the words "Peggy's. Good Cookin'. Good Eatin'."

Carley took an empty table for two and picked up the menu. Before she had time to read it fully, Kurt Lister stood beside her. She'd only seen him briefly that night at the restaurant with his wife, but the man was hard to forget. Tall and muscular, with a commanding air, he dominated the room. Gone was the hard, skeptical manner he had exhibited formerly. Today, he smiled at her as if they were the best of friends. His cropped hair, dark goatee, and an indefinable something she couldn't put a name to, gave an intriguing impression of hidden danger.

He motioned toward the other tables. "There doesn't seem to be room for me. May I join you?"

Carley glanced around the room. The place was full, of course, but there were a couple of other small tables like hers with only one person sitting there. She thought about saying so but decided it would be rude. "Of course."

Kurt sat down and reached for a menu. "It was nice meeting you the other night. I don't get over this way much, so I'm not acquainted with a lot of people. Have you lived here long?"

"All my life." Carley turned her attention back to the menu.

After the waitress left with their orders, Kurt leaned back in his chair and smiled, his dark gray business suit, wine-colored shirt, and black tie looking somewhat out of place with the jeans, cotton shirts, and sneakers worn by some of the other patrons. "So, are the police making any headway on catching the guy who shot your friend?"

Carley took a sip of water, not wanting to talk about Nancy but seeing no way to avoid it. "No, not yet. Or at least if they are, they haven't told me anything about it."

"Well, they probably wouldn't. Police are known for being close-mouthed, but they should keep you informed. It's rough on you not to know what's going on."

The smile and gentle tone of voice disarmed her. Why had she been so unsure of him to start with? Probably because she was leery of everyone and would be until the monster who killed Nancy had been captured. She needed to relax a little and not be so judgmental of people she didn't know very well.

The waitress arrived with their food: chicken and noodles and a salad for her, and ribs and sauerkraut for him. Carley waited until she left before responding.

"It is hard. The hardest part is realizing he seems to be after me, although I don't know why. My house has been broken into." She tried to keep her voice calm. Until she learned who her enemy was, she needed to stay strong and alert.

Kurt leaned toward her, his expression compassionate. "You don't have an alarm?"

"I do now."

Uh-oh. She probably shouldn't have told him that. The fewer people who knew about the alarm, the better. But Kurt probably couldn't care less whether she had one or not. She couldn't imagine this man sneaking around breaking into houses. If someone had something he wanted, he'd more than likely walk right up and demand it be handed over.

"That's good. An alarm is a fine thing to have. But if you need anything, give me a call. I'll be there as soon as I can make it." He drew a small leather case from his pocket and removed a card. "Here. Call any time. I'll be there."

Carley accepted the card, knowing she wasn't likely to call. It was nice of him to offer, but he had a wife who might be a little harder to deal with. From what she'd seen of Marlene Lister, she wouldn't take it well if some woman called her husband in the middle of the night to come help her. Better not take that route. It really *could* be dangerous. She smiled just thinking about it while spooning the last of the seasoned, richly flavored chicken and noodles.

He gave her a serious look. "I saw you with Blake Richards. I wouldn't think he'd be your type."

Carley's smile faded. "What do you mean, not my type?" And what business was it of his?

He shrugged and buttered a roll. "Oh, he's just so straitlaced, hooked on church, afraid to have fun. You come across as a woman who's ready to enjoy life."

Carley shook her head. "No, you're wrong about that. It's not my style at all."

He reached across the table and patted her hand, giving her that warm grin. "Sometimes we don't know what we're really like until we give ourselves a chance."

She moved her hand, not wanting to encourage him. The restaurant crowd had thinned out while they had been eating, but she still didn't want anyone to see him patting her hand and acting overly friendly. "No, that kind of life is not for me. I like things quiet and settled."

Kurt got to his feet, grinning at her. "Well, perhaps someone will come along and change your mind. I've enjoyed talking to you, Carley. Maybe we can have dinner together again some time."

He picked up both checks over her protests, smiled again, and left.

Carley glanced around the room and saw Blake sitting three tables away—he didn't look happy. She tried a tentative smile and got no response, but he did get up from the table, carrying his coffee cup, and moved to sit down across from her. She waited, wondering what he had in mind.

"I see you had dinner with Kurt Lister. He didn't waste much time, did he?"

"It's not what you think. The restaurant was full and he asked if he could sit here. I certainly didn't ask him to join me."

"I didn't say you did. I said *he* didn't waste any time. It would be a good idea to stay away from him. He's got a reputation."

"I told you, it wasn't my idea that he sat down here."

He had suggested they might get together for dinner sometime, but she had no intention of following through on that. Besides, it wasn't any of Blake's business either way. Carley felt a guilty pang of remorse at the thought. Blake had done so much for her. She needed to control her irritation and be a little easier to get along with. But just the same, he had no right to be so overbearing. He'd been telling her what to do ever since he had come to her rescue back at the park, and sometimes it grated on her nerves.

"A reputation for what?" she asked. "Surely not for cheating on the dragon lady? I'd think she'd have his hide for that."

"She would if she knew about it. Marlene's tough, but Kurt's pretty good at hiding his trail."

"Oh, come on. If you know about it, then probably others do too. Don't tell me you think the gossip machine in Westfield is broken down? Besides, I don't think she'd be that easy to fool."

He held up a hand. "Well, whether it's right or not, it's time to stop this. We can't accomplish anything by arguing over something that's not all that important. Has anything else happened?"

Carley took a few seconds to calm down before answering. After all, he was the one who had started this particular argument. He needn't act like it was her idea. "No, not yet, but I keep expecting something to go wrong. Unless this guy has finally realized that I don't know anything or have anything that might pertain to Nancy and her death."

"You're sure it's related to that?"

"What else could it be? No matter what you seem to think, I've lived a rather boring life. There's no reason for anyone to be after me." At least, it had been a lot quieter since her parents' death. She'd lost her taste for excitement.

"Well, someone thinks he has a reason to do this. We need to find out what's going on."

Carley agreed. They needed to come up with a plan to get it done. Which was turning out to be harder than she had expected. What would happen next?

Blake followed Carley home, thinking he shouldn't have said anything about Kurt. She was free to talk to anyone she wanted, and what she did was none of his business. And she was right. He didn't actually know anything about Kurt and Marlene, except for local gossip. He was just upset to see another man on friendly terms with Carley. What was wrong with him, acting this way? He'd always had a reasonable amount of common sense, but he seemed to have lost it since meeting this woman again. He needed to get himself under control and stop acting like a jealous jerk.

When he pulled into her driveway, she was waiting for him. He rolled down the window as she approached.

"I have an idea. I want to go out to the park where Nancy was killed, but I don't want to go alone. Will you go with me?"

"Why do you want to go out there? I'd think you'd want to avoid the place."

"I would like to avoid it, but I'm hoping it will help me remember the details of that night. It all happened so fast I could easily have forgotten something. But I'm not brave enough to go out there by myself."

He took a deep breath and gave the only answer he could give. "All right, I'll go with you. Get in. I'll drive."

She hurried around the car and got into the passenger seat. "I appreciate this. It may not help at all, but I have to try."

"No problem. It won't be so bad in daylight, and probably no one will be in that area of the park. You'll have plenty of time to look around."

He drove to Silver Oaks Park, taking the road Carley had used that night. She told him where to stop, and he pulled over to the side and shut off the motor. For a moment they just sat, looking around before getting out of the car. Blake glanced at the trees and shrubbery, nerves alert. No reason to think the killer was lurking somewhere, trying to ambush them, but he still felt on edge.

She stopped walking. "Nancy's car was right about here."

The weather had been dry, and a faint bloodstain was still visible. Carley hesitated beside it, blinking back tears. After a minute, she tilted her chin and moved to sit down on the bench located a little way back from the road and situated beneath a large oak.

She looked up at him, and he could see the strain in her expression. "This is where we were sitting when we heard him coming. Nancy jumped up and started to run, and he shot her. Then he started shooting at me."

Blake glanced around, amazed that Carley had escaped. "You must have run the instant he began."

"Nancy acted so strangely, I was already spooked. I heard the gunfire ... saw her fall, and I just panicked."

She looked so upset, he put his arm around her, pulling her against him. "Don't start thinking you were to blame for anything. The guy was determined to kill her, and there was nothing you could do to stop him. If he hadn't killed her then, he'd have murdered her eventually. Besides, you didn't have any way to defend yourself. Running was the best thing you could have done."

They sat there for a while, and Blake tried to steer the conversation into more general topics. Carley's answers showed she was still dwelling on what had happened that night. He finally gave up, just sitting quietly and watching her as she looked around, wearing an almost dazed expression. A car motor sounded in the distance, coming their way.

Carley leaped to her feet. "It's just like it was that night."

Blake stood with her, sure that the murder scene wasn't being reenacted, but ready to defend her whatever happened. A police car appeared, heading toward them. He relaxed for a moment, thinking it was just a routine patrol, but then he saw a handgun pointing out the window. Blake grabbed Carley by the shoulders and shoved her behind the trunk of the large oak tree standing in back of the bench. He dove after her just as gunshots ripped the air. Bullets slammed into the tree trunk where they had been standing before the car speeded up and disappeared around a curve in the road.

He pulled her toward his car. "Hurry!"

Blake turned the car around, peeled out, and headed back the way they had come. Carley peered out at the side mirror. "That was a police car. Why would the police be shooting at us?"

"I don't know, but I'm going to call Russ and see what's going on."

Carley grabbed his arm. "You can't call Russ. He's the police, and a policeman shot at us. You can't trust him right now."

Blake shook his head at her. "Look, Russ knows we're no threat to him or anyone else. He wouldn't have any reason to shoot at us or send someone to do it for him. We have to report this." He intended to learn the truth about whomever was behind these attacks. He wanted answers and he wanted them now.

Blake pulled into the first parking lot he came to and grabbed his cell phone. Russ answered on the second ring.

"What do you mean a cop shot at you? That's impossible."

"Look, I was there. It was a police car. I didn't get a look at the driver. I just saw the barrel of a gun and headed for cover."

"I know my men. Not one of them would pull a stunt like this. Where are you, anyway?"

"In the parking lot of Dollar General. Why?"

"You stay there. We're going back to the park, and you're going to show me some evidence of what you claim happened."

Blake clamped down on his anger. This was no time to start an argument or mouth off. "We'll wait here, but I don't like being called a liar. I was there. I know what I saw. I heard the shot. Heard the impact of the bullet. So I'll go back with you, but you get yourself under control before you get here. Got that?"

"Yeah, I got it. And I know we've been friends for a lot of years, but I still don't believe one of my guys shot at you."

He hung up and Blake glanced over at Carley. "He's coming. Wants us to take him back to where we were shot at. He doesn't believe us."

The look she gave him was hot enough to start a brush fire. "That's fair enough, since I don't trust him either. What's to keep him from taking us back there and then doing a better job this time?"

He shook his head, denying what she had just said. "Look, you can't really believe Russ would hurt us. You know him better than that. I don't know what's going on, but I trust him to be on our side."

"Right now, I'm careful who I trust. I've been attacked twice and that's enough. Maybe he was getting back with Nancy, and maybe he wasn't. I don't know what I believe right now."

A police car drove into the lot, and he gave her a serious look. "Give him a chance before you condemn him, okay?"

She didn't say anything, which was good because Russ pulled alongside Carley's side of the car and rolled his window down. "You follow me. We're going to check this out."

Blake nodded and started the motor, backing out and falling in behind the police car. He didn't care to return to the place where they'd been shot at. The park appeared deserted, but there were too many wooded areas to hide in. A light wind had picked up, rustling the tree limbs. Russ stopped at the spot where Nancy had been killed, got out of his police car, and leaned against the closed door. His lips were tight, his jaw lifted as if daring them to prove they were shot at. Blake parked behind him and glanced at Carley, not sure how she would react. "He wants us to get out."

She didn't answer, but she did open the car door, which he considered a small victory. Together they approached Russ. The cop didn't smile. "Now, where were you when this supposedly happened?"

Blake led the way to the bench and pointed at the wounds on the oak tree. "Right there. If we hadn't jumped behind that tree, we'd be dead by now."

Russ stared at the gouges on the tree for a moment and then dug out his pocket knife. He probed the bark and pried out a flattened bullet, turning it over in his hand. "I'm just guessing, but as near as I can tell, this could be the same caliber that killed Nancy. I don't know what happened here, but it looks like you were just plain lucky."

"You got that right." Blake could still hear the impact of the bullet against the tree. It had been a narrow escape.

Carley stared at the bullet in Russ' hand, face pale and eyes wide. Blake had a good idea what she was thinking. The same thing he was. That was too close for comfort. How could this be happening in a little town like Westfield?

Russ ran his thumb over the chunk of metal. "Okay, I apologize. You were shot at. It looks like one of my men is in trouble. There's no way anyone could have gotten his hands on a car without doing something to the cop inside. I've got a bad feeling about this."

Blake absorbed the words, finding he agreed with Russ. They were walking in the dark here. He knew the town policemen. Good men, all of them. Something definitely was wrong, and he had a feeling danger was moving ever closer. Only with God's help could they keep Carley safe.

Chapter Eight

Blake drove slowly through Westfield to where Rachel Blevins had lived. He found her address, parked in the driveway, and looked around. The woman's house, a two-story older home painted white with a green roof, sat back from the street. The yard was neatly mowed, and large pots filled with red geraniums flanked each side of the porch steps. A porch swing creaked in the light breeze.

Whatever else she had been, it was obvious Rachel had been meticulous about her home. From the pictures of her in the local papers, she had been a pretty woman—a woman with a life full of potential. She had been a nurse, well liked and respected. Like Nancy. So who had killed them and why? Both women had been destroyed before their time.

He saw a curtain twitch in the neighbor's window and got out of the car to walk across the lawn to her house. The door opened as soon as he rang the bell, so apparently the tall, gray-haired woman with the piercing hazel eyes had been watching him.

"Yes?"

Blake introduced himself. "I'm a friend of Nancy Wilkins, and I have reason to believe her death was connected to the death of Rachel Blevins. May I talk to you for a few minutes?"

The woman glanced around the neighborhood, but Blake knew no one was in sight. She had a right to be leery of him, and he didn't blame her for being cautious. He motioned toward the porch chairs. "We could sit out here if you prefer."

She nodded and stepped out on the porch. "What do you want to know?"

"Anything you can tell me about what Rachel was like and who might have had reason to hurt her. I'm just looking for information that might help the police."

The woman's face crumpled, and she sank into an old fashioned slat-backed rocker, clasping her hands in her lap. "She was a precious young woman. Always friendly, always willing to help anyone who needed anything."

Blake sat down in the other chair. "And yet someone killed her."

The woman wiped her eyes. "Yes, someone killed her. I'd sure like to see whoever did it caught and punished. My name is Lucille Matthews. I've lived next door to Rachel for these past four years. I can't believe she's gone. Particularly like that."

Blake leaned closer. "Can you think of anyone who might have done it? Anyone she was having a problem with?"

Lucille shook her head. "Rachel never had a problem with anyone. She was that sweet-natured. Always smiling, always laughing—she made every day brighter just by being there."

"There must have been something," Blake insisted. Someone had a reason for wanting to get rid of her.

Lucille hesitated, looking thoughtful. "There's been something different about her lately. I never saw anyone over there—a man, I mean—but for some months now she seemed a little preoccupied. She'd come home at odd hours or come in, then leave a short time later. She wasn't the type to see friends or go out a lot. It was so different from her usual behavior that I suspected she might have been seeing someone. Sometimes she'd seem happy, but then other times, she seemed sort of down and maybe a little angry."

Blake mulled this over in his mind. "So what do you think was going on?"

Lucille crimped her lips and glanced away from him, not speaking. Then her eyes met his. She heaved a sigh. "I guess I thought she was seeing a man, but he never came around here, never picked her up. Rachel was a beautiful woman. Any man should have been happy to be seen with her, so why didn't he come to her house to get her? Why didn't any of her neighbors ever see him?"

"And you're thinking what?" Blake had a good idea what she would say, but he wanted to hear it.

Lucille sighed again. "I hate saying it out like this, particularly since she's dead, but I couldn't help suspecting that maybe he had something to hide. That is, if I'm right and she was seeing someone."

"So why didn't he want to be seen?"

"There could have been several reasons, but the one that comes to mind is if he was already married and he was seeing Rachel behind his wife's back. And it hurts me to say it. It's hard to believe it of her. She wasn't that type."

Blake knew there was a good chance she was right. "We all slip up sometimes. Everyone has a past. That's why we need God."

Lucille nodded. "I know that, and even Christians can stumble and fall, but I loved that girl. I just can't bear thinking something like that about her."

"Was Rachel a Christian?"

"She was, but she had stopped going to church. I tried to talk to her about it, but she just changed the subject."

Blake paused to think about this. So a good, neighborly woman—a Christian—had changed and become secretive, hiding something. "Is there anyone she could have confided in? Someone she would have trusted enough to talk to?"

Lucille looked thoughtful. "Well, not in the neighborhood, I'm sure. We all look out for each other, but we're not as close as that."

"What about some friend her own age? Someone special to her?"

Her expression cleared. "Of course. I should have thought of Kara before. Kara Delano. She and Rachel grew up together. They talked almost every day. But I don't have her address. All I have is a telephone number Rachel gave me when she was out of town so I could call Kara if I needed anything since I'm a little unsteady on my feet. Sometimes I have to use a walker. It's good to have someone checking on me. Let me get the number for you."

Blake waited while she went into the house. This was a nice neighborhood. The houses were clean and well kept. Kids played on the sidewalk, and a middle-aged man sat on the front steps at the house two doors down, keeping an eye on them. Hard to imagine a killer touching the people who lived here. But then, no one was really safe, no matter where they lived. Evil could strike at any time, any place.

Lucille returned, holding out a slip of paper. "I found it. You can take it with you."

Blake took it and glanced at the number. He'd call her and see if she would talk to him. Maybe he'd take Carley with him so Kara wouldn't be nervous. Seeing a strange man at her door so soon after her friend's murder might make her a little more cautious.

He thanked Lucille and drove a few blocks, then he pulled into a parking lot to call Kara. He got her answering machine but didn't leave a message. It would be better if he talked with her.

A couple of hours after he got home, his cell phone rang. Russ. *Wonder what he wants.* "Yeah? What's up?"

"You busy right now?"

Blake glanced at his watch—7:00 p.m. and no, he wasn't busy. "Not especially. Why?"

"I want you to go over to Carley's. I have something to talk to the two of you about, and I'd just as soon do it with both of you together."

Something to talk to Carley about? What did this mean? Had they found the guy who killed Nancy, or was this something that would hurt Carley? Sure, he'd be at her house. Better believe it. "What time do you want me there?"

"In about ten minutes. Can you manage that?"

"No problem. I'll leave right now."

He pulled into the drive ahead of Russ. They walked to the door together, and Blake wished he'd gotten there earlier so he could have had a chance to talk to Carley instead of arriving with the police. He hoped she didn't get the wrong idea with both of them showing up at the same time.

Carley opened the door, her eyes widening when she saw the two of them. "Is anything wrong?"

Russ shook his head. "No, nothing like that. I just have something to tell you both, and this is the easiest way to do it. Can we sit down?"

"Of course." Carley led the way to the living room and took one of the armchairs. Blake sat down on the couch, which left the other chair for Russ.

He leaned forward, elbows resting on the chair arms. "I wanted to tell you that we found the police car the guy who shot at you was driving."

Blake narrowed his eyes, wondering what was coming next. He knew most of the guys on the police force. It was hard to imagine one of them pulling something like that, even though he'd seen the vehicle and knew it was a Westfield police car.

Russ waited, but when neither of them said anything, he went on. "The cop was inside. He'd been shot. He's in the hospital now, still unconscious."

Carley wet her lips. "Who is it?"

"Jason Laney. I don't know what happened. Jase would be hard to slip up on, but this guy managed it. And Jase can't tell us what happened."

Blake thought of what Russ wasn't saying. Maybe Jason never would be able to tell them.

Carley stared at Russ. "Why would anyone go to all that trouble to try to kill me? Why is he doing this?"

Russ shook his head. "I don't know. But he must think you're some kind of threat to him. He must have a lot to lose to take a chance like this. If he'd messed up with Jase, he could be in jail right now. Jase is tough to handle. I'm surprised this guy could take him down."

"But how can I be a threat to him? I don't even know who he is."

She looked so incredulous Blake had to believe her. So who was this guy and why was he after Carley? "If this is the guy Nancy saw at the restaurant, then he has to wonder if she told Carley about him. He's killed two women and he's facing serious prison time if he gets caught."

Russ nodded. "Yeah, that probably has something to do with why he'd be after her. He may think she could identify him. The one person who could put him in that prison with her testimony."

"But I didn't see him, and she didn't give me his name."

"He has no way of knowing that," Russ pointed out.

"Well, I'd certainly like to make him aware of it. How's Marianne doing? She and Jason have two little kids."

"It's rough on her. Marianne's holding up, but you can see she's taking it hard."

"Is she at the hospital or at home?"

"She's at the hospital. Her mother is taking care of the kids. You thinking of going to see her?"

Carley nodded. "Yes, I am. Do you have any objections?"

"No. I think it would be good. She needs all the help she can get right now."

"I'll call Mildred Horner and ask her to put them on the prayer chain."

"You do that." Russ got to his feet. "Well, that's all I had to say. Guess I'd better get busy. You keep in touch."

Blake walked him to the door and locked it behind him. He went back to the living room to find Carley waiting for him.

She shot him a look that held a world of challenge. "I'm going to the hospital to see Marianne."

"Not by yourself, you're not. I'm going with you. When do you want to go?"

"Right now."

Carley left the room for a few minutes, then returned, pulling on a dark blue jacket that matched her eyes and looked great with her jeans and white cable-knit sweater. She set the alarm, and as they walked out to the cars, he motioned toward his dark blue Ford. "I'm driving."

Blake thought for a moment she would protest, but after a second's hesitation, she got into the front passenger seat. A few minutes later they pulled into the parking lot of the community hospital. Carley had the door open almost before he stopped. Blake got out and looked around, checking the parked cars to make sure it was safe before following her into the hospital. He didn't really expect to be ambushed here, but it paid to be careful.

Carley halted at the information desk where Destiny Owens, a friend of hers, was on duty, and asked where she could find Marianne Laney. Destiny faced them, tears welling in her eyes. "She's in the waiting room. The doctors are still with him, and he may be sent by ambulance to a bigger hospital. Go down that way and take the first right. You'll find the emergency room waiting room just around the corner."

They thanked her and started down the hall, Carley in the lead. She didn't realize how fast she was walking until Blake caught her by the arm. "Hey, wait a minute. If you go running in like this, you're liable to scare Marianne. Slow down and walk normally. She's got enough to deal with without us bursting in on her."

After a moment, she nodded. "I'm worried about her, but you're right. I'll take it a little slower."

They turned the corner and entered the ER's waiting room and found Marianne, a little taller than Carley and with dark hair brushing her shoulders, sitting with her head down, hands clasped in her lap. It looked like she was praying. Carley took the time to breathe a short prayer of her own that God would take care of Jason and his family. The young cop was probably in his early thirties—a lot of life ahead of him if he survived this. She rethought that. No one was guaranteed a long life. It was in God's hands, like everything else, but she'd keep them both in her prayers.

Marianne glanced up and stood to face them. Carley stepped forward, arms reaching out. "Marianne, we came as soon as we learned what happened. Are you all right?"

She sagged into Carley's arms, holding her tight for a moment. "Oh, Carley. Russ said someone shot at you from Jason's car. He didn't do it. He wouldn't have done something like that."

"I know. We heard that he'd been hurt. How is he?"

"He's still unconscious. The doctors don't say much. I guess there isn't really much to tell. He's just lying there, and all I can do is pray."

"That's the best thing you can do. And I've called Mildred. She's alerting the prayer chain."

Marianne gripped her arm. "Oh, thank you. I was so upset I never thought of that. I appreciate it so much."

"And if you or the kids need anything, let us know. We'll do everything we can to help."

Carley brushed Marianne's curls back from her forehead. Usually impeccable with her clothes and with makeup perfect, today Marianne was rumpled, her hair falling in disarray. The jeans and lavender shirt with a couple of food stains on it showed she hadn't taken time to change, and she looked worried sick. It wasn't good for her to be here alone. Carley decided to call some of the women from the church and organize volunteers to be with Marianne—someone to talk to, to pray with, to just be there for her in case she needed something.

She and Blake stayed for about an hour, and then Carley got to her feet and pulled her friend into a hug. "Try to get some rest. If you need me, I'll stay with you. Just say the word."

Marianne shook her head. "I'll be all right. And Russ has promised to send a man to stand guard outside. He said he didn't expect the person who shot Jason to come here, but he wanted to be sure he was safe."

Carley sucked in a frightened breath. She hadn't thought about that. Could Jason identify the man who attacked him? If so, he would be a danger to a person who had already killed twice. She glanced at Blake, seeing the same thought reflected in his eyes. The man causing all this havoc would destroy anyone who got in his way.

Blake drove Carley home and insisted on coming in with her. "Don't even argue. I'm not going to stay, but I am going to check out this house before I leave you alone. Okay?"

She stared at him for a minute, trying to be angry but failing. "All right."

It was good of him, and she knew she had to get over this "I'll do it myself" attitude and be grateful someone was interested in helping her. After what had happened in the park, and what that creep had done to Jason, she needed to stop being so determined to hold people at arm's length.

She followed Blake through the house as he checked behind doors and in closets. When he was sure everything was safe, he walked to the front door, then stopped, looking down at her. "Lock the door behind me, and don't open it to anyone unless you know who they are and you're sure you can trust them."

Carley nodded. "I will. Thank you for checking out everything."

He looked down at her, grinning. "You're thanking me? You're not going soft on me, are you? What happened to Miss I-Can-Do-It-Myself?"

"Maybe she's growing up." Carley grinned back, thinking how good it was to have him here looking down at her like she was something special. No one had looked at her that way in a long time. The thought saddened her. Blake might not be so friendly when he learned the truth about her. She wasn't as nice as he believed.

She heard her phone buzz as she closed and locked the door after Blake. Someone was texting her. She read the message and froze.

I SAW YOU AT THE HOSPITAL, BUT YOU DIDN'T SEE ME. YOU CAN RUN, BUT YOU CAN'T HIDE.

Chapter Nine

Carley stared at the words. He saw her at the hospital? She hadn't noticed anyone, but she'd been intent on getting to Marianne. Who was this man, and why was he doing these things? Did he really believe she had seen him in the park when he shot Nancy?

She closed her eyes and forced her thoughts back to that horrible moment when her world had exploded with the shot that killed her best friend. All she could remember was the car, and the blast from the gun rupturing the quiet of the night. Then she was running for her life, dodging trees and bushes, expecting every moment to have a bullet slam into her back.

She called Russ to tell him about the text message. He dropped by and looked at it, concern evident in his brown eyes. "Did you see anyone that caught your attention? Someone watching you?"

"No, but I was concentrating on Marianne and Jason. I really wasn't paying that much attention to anyone else."

"Okay, we'll check it out, but you need to be careful. This guy is serious trouble. Don't you have someplace you can stay until we catch him?"

"I don't want to put anyone else in danger. Like you said, he's serious trouble, and evidently he knows where I am. He could follow me wherever I go. I stayed at a motel the other night, but I feel safer in my own house."

"Okay, it's up to you, but you call the minute something doesn't feel right. Don't wait until you know for sure something's wrong. If you feel uneasy, call."

He left and Carley went through the nightly routine of checking the alarm, locking the doors, and closing the drapes. But she still didn't feel safe. Later, in bed and trying to sleep, she realized she was lying stiff, muscles tight and nerves on edge, straining to hear, as if she expected someone to break in. Finally, she did what she should have done in the first place—she prayed, turning it over to God, trusting Him to take care of her. At last she felt at ease enough to close her eyes and welcome sleep.

The next morning, she didn't hear the alarm and woke twenty minutes past her usual time. She felt as limp as a wrung-out dishrag. This constant pressure was wearing her down. Something had to break soon. After a hasty breakfast, she got ready for work, arriving five minutes late. She booted her computer and got busy, glad Mr. Quigley hadn't seen her. He was almost a fanatic about being punctual. The door to his office was closed, so either he wasn't in or he was talking on the phone. Either way was all right with her, as long as he wasn't looming over her desk, staring at her in the intense way he had developed. It gave her the creeps.

As if her thoughts had summoned him, he opened the door and started toward her desk. "Miss Sutherland, I have something I want you to do for me. There's a meeting in Oldham I need you to attend. I'd send Miss Osborn, but I need her here."

Carley stared at him. Was this a ploy to ease her into taking Nancy's job? No matter, she couldn't see any way out of this. At least it would get her out of the office for the day. "All right. Give me the address. What time do I need to be there?"

"You have an hour and a half. Get Miss Osborn to brief you on what you need to do. I'll get someone to fill in for you on your job."

He turned on his heel and strode back to his office while Carley watched, stunned. That was it? Just talk to Juanita and go. It seemed strange after the way he'd been behaving, but it was definitely a relief. She spent ten minutes talking to Juanita Osborn and then headed out for the meeting.

On the way to Oldham, she kept glancing at her rearview mirror and watching the side roads, nerves on edge. Would a black SUV suddenly appear, trying to force her off the road? She'd never been the nervous type, but she had become constantly alert, jumping at the slightest noise, afraid to trust anyone. Except Blake. It was hard living this way.

After sitting through the meeting and taking notes on what, to her, seemed like an unnecessary waste of time, Carly headed for home. Heavy traffic slowed her down. She stopped at a red light and glanced in her rearview mirror, noticing a black SUV a few cars behind. A chill crept through her but she tried to dismiss it. After all, there were probably several vehicles like that in the area. What were the chances it would be the man who had killed Nancy? Still, she kept an eye on the car. As it gradually crept closer in the line of traffic, she grew more nervous. The light in front of her turned yellow as she approached, but she scooted through before it became red. With the SUV stuck at the light, she speeded up as much as possible and whipped onto a side road. From there, she kept dodging onto one street after another until she was out of Oldham. She drove past the steep dropoff where someone had tried to drive Nancy off the road. No one could have survived going over that cliff. Whoever had tried to push Nancy's car off there had intended to kill her. No wonder her friend had been so upset.

At the end of the day she parked in her own driveway with a sigh of relief. It was good to get home. She unlocked her front door, then turned to face the street just as a black SUV drove by. The vehicle slowed to a crawl, but the driver's face was covered with a black stocking cap with holes cut for eyes.

Carley opened the door and stumbled inside, locking it behind her. A glance out the window showed the SUV was gone. Was it the same car she had seen in Oldham? He hadn't been able to follow her. She was sure of that. Besides, she had spent some time at the office. Surely he wouldn't have known where to find her after she'd lost him that morning.

Who was this man and why hadn't the police been able to catch him? She slumped into the nearest chair, realizing she was trembling. He was going to drive her into a heart attack—if he didn't kill her first.

Blake phoned Kara Delano, hoping she would be home. Not that he expected to learn much, but he had to try. She answered on the fourth ring.

He introduced himself and explained what he wanted. Kara was silent. Blake tried again. "Look, I'm not a reporter or the police. I'm a friend of Nancy Wilkins, who was killed last week. I think she knew something about Rachel's murder. I'm just trying to find out the truth."

There was a long pause. "How do I know you're who you say you are? After all, Rachel was killed. Maybe you had a hand in that."

"Hey, no. That's not true. I'm just a guy who knew Nancy, and now the killer is after Carley Sutherland. She was with Nancy when she was killed, and she's had some serious problems lately that could be connected. I guess he thinks she might have seen him. I'm trying to help her."

Silence.

"Kara?"

"I'm thinking. How about you bring this woman with you this evening? I'll have a friend here too. I'll feel safer that way."

"It's a deal." Blake glanced at his watch. Six o'clock. Carley should be home by now. "Say in half an hour?"

"Make it seven o'clock. That will give me time to set it up."

Set it up? Well, he guessed he'd have to go along with whatever she planned if he wanted to talk to her. "Seven it is."

Blake hung up the phone and called Carley, telling her about the appointment with Kara and asking her to go with him. She sounded incredulous. "She's a friend of Rachel Blevins? You think she'll know something about who the killer might be?"

"I don't know," he admitted. "But I don't think we can afford to give it a pass."

After a pause she said, "All right. What time are you picking me up?"

"About a quarter till. That okay?"

"I'll be ready."

Yes, she'd be ready. Carley was dependable. He was learning more about her all the time, and she was becoming more important to him every day. Carley was a woman now, and he burned with the desire to develop a deep personal relationship with her.

Even as the feeling hit him, his thoughts turned to Afghanistan and his friend Lee Bordman. He and Lee had grown up together and enlisted a few months apart. Had been in the same unit until a roadside bomb took his friend's life. Blake was riding in the Humvee behind the one Lee was in when the bomb went off. He'd never forget the explosion, the flying debris. In an instant, his friend was gone.

Lee had just learned he was a father to a baby boy before they went on that mission. He couldn't wait to get back home and see his son.

But he would never see that baby, and that little boy would grow up without doing things with his dad, without building a relationship with who would have been the most important man in his life. Many important experiences and memories had been taken from that little boy.

Blake had paid a visit to Lee's wife, Lana, after getting home from Afghanistan. Their son was a perfect baby boy, and Lee would have been proud of him. Lana's gaunt, tearstained face, red-rimmed eyes, and thin figure accented her sadness. Every word she said was tinged with grief. Blake knew he could never put a woman he loved through what Lana was dealing with.

He was attracted to Carley, but he needed to be careful and not let it go further than that. Better to wait until he was home for good, and then, if she was still available, he could do something about it.

Blake showed up at Carley's door five minutes early to find her ready and waiting. Before he could get out of the car, she was through the door and locking it behind her. He waited patiently until she climbed into the passenger seat, asking questions.

"How did you find this Kara person?"

He told her about Rachel's neighbor and the information she gave him. "So this friend may be able to tell us something. At least it's worth a try."

"I guess it is." Carley leaned back and fastened her seat belt. "Thanks for asking me to come with you."

Blake laughed. "She refused to see me unless I brought you along, and she'll have a friend with her. I got the idea she didn't trust me."

"Somehow, that makes me feel better. If she'd been pushing to talk with you, I'd be a little suspicious."

"No, this was my idea, not hers." Blake pulled into the driveway of a medium-sized, cream-colored ranch house and looked over at Carley. "Well, this is it. Let's go see what we can learn."

They walked toward the front of the house and rang the bell. The door opened to reveal a man with fairly long, sandy hair and a shaggy goatee. He had a gold stud in his left ear, and the blue tee shirt he wore revealed a well-muscled chest. A tattoo of an eagle covered his upper left arm. The guy looked tough. "Yeah?"

"Blake Richards and Carley Sutherland. We have an appointment with Miss Delano."

"Right. I'm Nate Douglas. She's waiting for you. Come on in."

Kara was slender with shining golden-brown hair falling past her shoulders and smoky brown eyes. She wore jeans and a lavender sweater. She smiled at them from a dark blue Queen Anne chair. They sat down on the couch, and Nate took the second chair.

After a heartbeat of silence, Kara spoke, her eyes on Blake. "What do you think I can do to help you?"

"You knew Rachel Blevins?"

She swallowed, blinking her eyes. "She was my best friend. It's like a big part of my life is missing."

Carley leaned forward. "I know what you mean. Nancy Wilkins was my best friend."

Kara narrowed her eyes. "What does that have to do with Rachel?"

"Nancy was in The Old Mill the night Rachel was murdered. She saw a man and woman together. They seemed to be arguing. The next day, she saw the woman's picture in the paper. It was Rachel. Her body had been found in a ditch."

Kara leaned forward, her body tense, eyes sharp and direct. "Could your friend describe the man?"

Carley shook her head. "She was killed before she could tell me. Since then, my house has been broken into, someone has been texting me threatening messages, and I've had phone calls. I'm sure it's the same man who killed Nancy and maybe killed Rachel."

"I see." Kara slumped back in the chair and sighed. "So what do we do now?"

Blake spoke up for the first time. "We need to find out more about this man. Did Rachel tell you anything about him?"

"Oh, yes, she told me," Kara said bitterly, "but nothing that will help. She never gave me a name or a description. All I know is that he talked her into seeing him in secret. He must be something special, because Rachel wasn't that kind of woman. I don't know how he convinced her to get involved with him."

"What do you mean she wasn't that kind?"

"She had values, and she lived by them. She wouldn't have gone out with another woman's husband without a good reason. Or what seemed like a good reason to her."

"What kind of reason do you have in mind?" Blake glanced at Nate, then shifted his attention back to Kara.

"Okay, I don't like saying this, but she told me the man was married but he was getting a divorce. That he was unhappy in his marriage. He loved her and he wanted to marry her."

Nate snorted. "And she fell for that? That's one of the most common tricks guys like this play."

"Rachel didn't have much experience with men," Kara said. "Her parents were very strict, and after she grew up, she was so concentrated on her career she didn't have time to date. I tried to get her to lighten up, but when she finally did, it proved to be a disaster."

"Did she tell you anything that could help identify him?" Carley leaned forward, drawing Kara's attention. "Anything personal?"

"No, but I think along toward the end, she was starting to realize he had no intention of leaving his wife or of marrying her. She was moody and irritable, like something was bothering her. I got the feeling things weren't going well."

"You think she was putting pressure on him?" Nate asked. "Pushing him to marry her?"

"After what happened to her, I'm fairly sure of it."

"And maybe she pushed too hard," Blake said. "It makes sense."

"And he killed her to shut her up." Nate nodded. "I can see that happening. Guy felt like he had to protect himself, so he got rid of her."

"I tried to talk to her about it—told her it was wrong—and she said she knew it was, but it would be all right in the end because he had told her it would be." Kara wiped her eyes. "I keep thinking I should have done more, but what could I do? I couldn't make her listen."

"You did all you could." Nate placed his hand on her shoulder. "Don't start blaming yourself. None of this is your fault. You knew Rachel. She wouldn't have made the first step. This guy had to have convinced her it would be all right. You said yourself she didn't have much experience. She would have been easy to fool."

"I know, but…"

"But nothing. You did what you could. She wouldn't listen and now it's too late."

Blake had a hunch Nate was right. It could have very well played out that way. They had to find the man who had won Rachel Blevins' heart and then destroyed her. Which might not be all that easy. Evidently, he had put a lot into keeping anyone from seeing him or learning anything about him. Blake needed to talk to Russ about this. "Can you think of anything else?"

Kara shook her head. "Not at this time. I'll think about it, and if anything occurs to me, I'll get in touch. Leave me your phone numbers."

They exchanged numbers, and Carley and Blake got up to leave. Kara reached out to hug Carley. "We both suffered a loss. I'll be praying for you."

"And I'll pray for you. What about Rachel's family?"

"Her parents died in a small plane crash, and she didn't have sisters or brothers. She was pretty much alone. There were a couple of cousins who came to the funeral, but that was about it."

Carley patted her arm. "Then we'll pray for each other. I'm glad I had this chance to meet you and talk to you. Let's stay in touch."

"I'd like that."

"Would you mind talking to Russ Pryor? He's the chief of police and in charge of this case." Blake knew not everyone felt comfortable talking to the police, and judging from the tough impression he got from Nate's appearance and manner, Kara might reject the idea.

"I'll be glad to talk to him anytime. I want this person caught."

Nate came to stand beside Kara, placing his arm around her. "We'll both do anything we can to help. Rachel didn't deserve to die like that. She was a fine woman. She just got in over her head with a guy who wasn't good enough for her."

Blake figured that pretty well summed it up. He shook hands with Nate and Kara, then led the way to the car. Carley eased into the passenger seat, looking disappointed. "Well, we know a little more than we did, but nothing that points to anyone as a suspect. No one seems to know anything about this guy."

Blake wanted to assure her they would find him, but she knew how narrow their chances were, so she probably wouldn't believe him. "Don't give up. Every little bit helps. Now we have to talk to Russ. He'll probably be ticked because we didn't call and let her talk to the police first, but he'll get over it."

It helped that Russ was an old friend. He would always put being a policeman first, but maybe he'd cut them some slack on this. Blake would just have to make the call and take the heat. No way around it.

Carley sat silently, thinking of Kara. They needed to stay in touch. Maybe they could help each other, and she would definitely be praying. She thought of what they had learned from that conversation. Poor Rachel, led astray by a man's lies and paying a horrible price for her sins. Was she a Christian? She would ask Kara. At least she knew Nancy was with God, which was a great comfort.

Having Blake beside her was a comfort too. The way she felt about him was nothing like the attraction she had felt in high school. They were adults, and her feelings went deeper and stronger than a high school crush. What was she going to do about that? He was healing more every day. Soon he'd be going back to Afghanistan, and she would have to make a choice about opening her heart to Blake. Was it worth the risk?

How did all those women handle watching the men they loved go off to war, knowing they might never come home? She felt a new compassion for the wives and families left behind. Of course, she and Blake didn't have the bonds of love and marriage other military couples had, but she was drawing closer to him all the time. She hated to see him go back to a dangerous place like Afghanistan.

Blake stopped in her driveway. "You want to go to the police station to talk to Russ, or you want to have him come here?"

Carley didn't have to think about that. "Have him come here. He's probably going to yell at us and at least here, it will be private."

Blake grinned. "You got that right. He's going to be riled, but he'll get over it. Let's go inside and call him."

Carley fixed them glasses of iced tea while they waited for Russ to arrive. It felt natural and good to just sit there talking instead of being forced to be alert every second, struggling to survive. Would they ever be allowed to live in peace?

When Russ came, she brought him a glass of tea. He took a hearty gulp and gave Blake a stern glance. "Okay, start talking. What's this all about?"

Blake shrugged. "I was just looking around, asking questions, and I talked to Rachel Blevins' next door neighbor. She gave me the name of a woman who had been Rachel's best friend. I called her and made an appointment to see her."

"Instead of telling me about it? I guess you didn't think of that."

"I didn't at the time. Later I knew you would probably be upset, so that's why I called you."

"Probably? You thought I would *probably* be upset? You knew I would be."

"Well, yeah, when I stopped to think about it. But she's willing to talk to you anytime."

"That's nice." Sarcasm dripped from his words. "I did talk to the neighbor, but she didn't give me any names to follow up on. So what did you learn, if you don't mind telling me?"

"I don't mind at all." Blake related all they'd learned from Kara and what Nate had said. By the time he had finished, Russ had calmed down and was taking notes.

"So they think she hooked up with a married guy who didn't want her making waves, so he got rid of her. You know, I'm having a hard time believing that's all that's involved. Divorce is common these days. I can't see that's any reason to kill twice and do his best to kill again. There's got to be more going on than we know so far. You have the number and address of the woman who told you this? I'll need to give her a call."

Blake provided the information, and Carley watched as Russ wrote it down. It wasn't much, but with God's help, maybe it would bring them one step closer to finding this person who had killed two decent women just because they had gotten in his way. If only Nancy had lived long enough to give a description of him. A new thought struck her.

"Russ, did you find Nancy's phone? She said she took a picture of the man with Rachel."

"No, I didn't. Her purse wasn't in the car and neither was her phone. If she had it with her, then someone must have taken it."

"It must be there. She had it with her that night. She was going to show it to me, but then the guy drove up and shot her."

Carley could close her eyes and still see that horrible picture burned in her mind—Nancy springing from the bench, the shot blasting, and her body slumping to the ground. Nothing Carley could do would erase it.

"Okay, I'll ask around. I can't believe we could have overlooked something like that, but I was shocked to find Nancy dead. It cut deep and I wasn't thinking as straight as I should have been." He got to his feet and looked at Blake. "I'll follow up on this, but the next time you get a bright idea, talk to me first."

"I'll do that," Blake said.

Carley took that with a grain of salt. From what she knew of him, Blake would act first and handle the fallout later. He was definitely a man of action. "One more thing, Russ. I was in Oldham at a meeting. Someone in a black SUV followed me. I managed to avoid him, but when I got home, the same car drove past my house, slowly, and the driver had something over his face, like a mask."

Russ stared at her. "You get a license number or anything?"

"No, nothing like that, and I haven't seen it since, but I thought you might want to know." She'd been watching for a car like that. So far, it hadn't shown up again.

"Yeah, I want to know, but that doesn't give me much to go on. If anything happens, you get on the phone. We'll keep an eye out for him, but there are several cars like that around. It'll be difficult to pinpoint the one that followed you without any other information." He left, and Carley stared at the window, thinking.

No, there wasn't much to go on and she hadn't seen the car again, but someone was after her. She could feel it in her bones. He could strike at any moment, and she would never see it coming.

Chapter Ten

Carley answered the door to find Kara standing there. A pink sweatshirt offset her golden-brown hair that was pulled back with an iridescent gold and burgundy clasp. Carley realized again how attractive she was. She also noticed the jerky movements and the way Kara kept glancing around the neighborhood as if looking for something.

Carley smiled, wondering about the reason for this visit. "Hi, Kara. Good to see you. Come on in."

Kara glanced around again before stepping inside quickly and closing the door behind her. Carley took a hasty look out the window at the street and neighboring houses but didn't see anything out of order. She motioned toward a chair. "What's up?"

Kara chose a seat away from the window. She hesitated. "I need to talk to you. Something has come up."

Carley sat down, feeling apprehensive. Something about Rachel? About the killer? Those were the only things she had in common with Kara. She waited, wondering what was wrong.

Kara heaved a sigh, her smoky-brown eyes still wary. "I've been getting phone calls."

"What kind of phone calls? Who are they from?"

"I don't know who it is. But they're scary. He says for me to stop talking to the police because if I don't, something bad will happen to me. Says he knows where I live. I didn't have this trouble before I talked to you."

Carley stared thoughtfully at her. "How did he know we talked? I haven't told anyone. Have you?"

"No, and I'm sure Nate didn't either. He's not one to talk much, particularly if it's something personal or pertains to me."

"I know Blake didn't discuss it either. So if no one else knew about it, how did he find out?" They'd told Russ, but surely he would be safe. Russ wouldn't tell anyone, would he? She dismissed the question. Of course he wouldn't.

Kara slumped in her chair. "So we don't have any idea who it could be. That's scary too. It's gotten to where I'm afraid to answer the phone."

Carley got up. "Let me get us something to drink, and we'll think this through. You want tea or Pepsi?"

"Pepsi, I guess."

Carley filled the glasses and carried them to the living room. "Have you thought of anything that might tell us something about this man Rachel was seeing?"

"No, but there was a man who pestered her a lot last year. He kept hanging around, pushing her for a date, but Rachel was sort of afraid of him. He was too aggressive, too possessive, didn't want her seeing anyone else. I don't know… There was something that just didn't seem right about him. I didn't like him from the beginning. It was a relief when he quit coming around."

Carley sipped at her drink. "Who was he?"

"Phil Peterson. You probably don't know him."

"Oh, don't I? He used to have a crush on Nancy. In fact, they did go out together a few times. Like you said, he was too possessive. Got upset if she talked to another guy, tried to keep her away from her family and friends. I talked her into breaking up with him, and he came unglued. Threatened her, promised to get even with me. It was a little wild for a while, but he gradually calmed down, or maybe he met someone else."

"Or maybe he met Rachel." Kara ran a finger down the beads of water on her glass, looking thoughtful. "She never dated him, but the situation was still kind of nasty. I know she was scared of him, and I wasn't comfortable around him either. Finally, he just went away."

"Not far enough away. I saw him recently, and he didn't look happy to see me again. Maybe the guy we want isn't the man she was seeing. It may be someone she knew before. Someone like Phil."

From what she had seen of Phil, he just might be dangerous if pushed too far. But as far as she knew, he wasn't married—and if he wasn't, their idea that the killer was cheating on his wife and killed Rachel to hide their relationship would be eliminated. So maybe they were on the wrong track. Could this be about revenge—Phil getting angry because he'd been rejected and making Rachel pay? Getting even with Nancy too? And he had promised to take care of Carley for talking Nancy into breaking up with him. Something to think about, anyway.

Kara shook her head, looking unconvinced. "That's possible, I guess, but we can't be sure. The thing is, Rachel was sort of innocent. Her dad was overly strict, wouldn't let her do things other kids could do. I mean, I'm a Christian, but he was too religious, if you know what I mean. He had a lot of rules—not God's rules, but his own rules. She had to do what he said and wasn't allowed to use her own judgment. From what she said, Rachel always resented it. She finally broke away and was enjoying her freedom before they died, but she still had that background of letting someone else make decisions for her."

"So we're looking for a man who can be overwhelming, maybe a bit of a bully. It may not be Phil but someone similar."

Apparently she and Rachel were opposites. She had been headstrong, determined to do what she pleased, refusing to listen to anyone. But it sounded as if she and Rachel had both gone to extremes in different directions and paid for it. Rachel had lost her life, and Carley had almost destroyed hers.

Kara nodded. "That's what I believe, and I think we're looking for the man she was seeing. Keeping him a secret wouldn't have been Rachel's idea. That wasn't like her. It sounds like he was the one with the most to lose."

"Okay, that's something to add to our list." A list that was still woefully short.

Kara fiddled with her watchband, her eyes downcast. "Blake seems nice. I guess you two are an item?"

An item? Not hardly, or at least not yet. "We're just friends. What about you and Nate?" *Friends. Carley wanted more, but that wasn't likely to happen.*

Kara sighed. "I care for Nate ... a lot, but his lifestyle is too different from mine. He wants things from me that I can't give. Right now, it doesn't look like he plans to change."

Carley nodded in sympathy. "I'm so sorry. It's hard, isn't it?"

"Very hard. I know I need to walk away from him, and maybe someday I will, but I keep hoping he'll get his life together. I don't really want to give up on him, but right now it wouldn't work out for the two of us."

Changing was hard. Carley knew from experience. She'd been there, but God could change even the most stubborn individual. She'd add Kara and Nate to her prayer list. "What are you going to do about the phone calls? Are you planning to tell the police?"

Kara's voice quivered. "No. I'm afraid to. He said for me to stay away from them. And he seems to know what I'm doing, where I'm going, or where I've been. It's like he's watching me, but I've never seen him."

Carley thought about that. Yes, that was exactly the way it was. As if he knew all about them—Kara, Blake, and her. Knew where they had been, what they'd done, who they had seen. It was more than a little spooky.

Somehow they had to break his cover. But how did they do that when they had no idea who he was?

Blake stopped at the Fas-Trip to fill up with gas. He didn't notice the guy at the next pump until he spoke. Nate Douglas. Kara's friend.

Nate inserted the nozzle into the tank of his car and leaned against his white Ford pickup. "So how are things going with you and Carley? Had any more problems?"

Blake shook his head. "Not yet, but I'm sure there will be. I've been doing some snooping on my own, but I've not found out much. If Rachel was seeing some guy, they had to have been really careful. No one seems to know anything about him."

Nate nodded. "I've been doing a little looking myself, but I've not had any luck either. I've got a feeling we'd better find something soon. Kara's been getting threatening phone calls. Got her really upset. I think she's in danger. Your woman is too."

His woman? Blake hadn't really thought of Carley that way, but he liked the sound of it. "So, is Kara your woman?"

"That's what I want, but she's got all these hang-ups about right and wrong. Goes to church, all of that stuff. Too straitlaced for me. Unless she loosens up, I can't see any hope for us. But that doesn't mean I can walk away when she's in trouble." Nate's hands curled into fists. "If I get hold of that jerk, I'll teach him a lesson he won't forget."

Blake figured in the mood he was in, Nate might do some serious damage to the guy and maybe end up in jail himself. He looked a little rough and acted it too. Somehow he didn't seem like a good match for Kara. She might be better off if they did break up. "The police are working on it, and maybe one of us will get lucky and find out something."

The pump clicked off, and he topped the tank and followed Nate inside to pay the cashier. When they returned to their vehicles, Nate nodded. "Good talking to you. If you come across any information, let me in on it, will you? I'll do the same with you."

Blake nodded. "Maybe we'll turn up something. I hope so, anyway."

He got in his car and drove away, wondering how the killer had traced them to Kara. It was like he knew everywhere they went. But who would have that kind of information? Russ? He was a cop, a trusted friend. Russ wouldn't be involved in this mess. He pushed the thought away, but it lingered in the back of his mind.

His cell phone rang and it was Russ, as if Blake's thoughts had summoned him. "Hey, I saw you talking to Nate Douglas. Learn anything new?"

Blake froze. He saw them? So where was he, and how come they didn't see him? He put the thought into words. "Where were you?"

"I drove by while you were filling your tanks."

Really? "I guess we didn't see you."

"Probably because I was driving my old red pickup. It's been around a while, nothing that would attract much attention. I still like to drive it occasionally to keep it running. So, did you learn anything new?"

Okay, the old pickup wouldn't catch their eye the way a police car would. Blake hesitated, then decided it wouldn't hurt to tell him. "Nate said Kara is getting harassing phone calls, threatening her if she talks to you again."

"Ah-huh. Wonder how he knew she'd talked to me?"

"That's what I was wondering."

"You or Carley didn't tell anyone, did you?"

"No, we didn't, and Nate said he and Kara didn't either. That leaves you."

"Not exactly. I parked in her driveway for about an hour. Someone could have seen me. A cop car is hard to hide."

Blake thought about that. It made sense. And besides, he didn't want to believe Russ was involved. "I guess that's probably what happened. So you think it's someone who lives close to her neighborhood?"

"I don't know what I think right now. But anything's possible. We're working on it. He'll mess up somewhere and we'll catch him."

"I'm glad you're so optimistic. I hope you're right, but I have to admit it doesn't look all that likely."

"Never say never. Listen, I need to go. I'll catch you later."

Russ hung up, and Blake realized he had driven to Carley's street. Since he was already here, he might as well stop in and check on her. Nothing more than that. It had nothing to do with wanting to see her.

Carley answered the door, her eyebrows lifted in an expression of surprise. "Hey, Carley. I was just driving by and decided to stop by and check on you."

"I'm fine. Kara was here, but she left a few minutes ago."

"I saw Nate down at the gas station. He told me she was getting phone calls, but he didn't tell me she was here."

"He may not have known."

They sat down in the living room, and Blake thought how natural it seemed to be there with her, as if he belonged. When they were together like this, he could see the possibility of them becoming a couple. Maybe even married—having children, together for always. That would be heaven on earth.

"Kara and I talked about Rachel. She knew Phil Peterson too. Apparently,

Rachel never went out with him the way Nancy did, but he hung around, pestering her for a date. So that's a connection between the two of them. You know him—he's got a temper and he's not into forgiving. In fact, from the way he glared at me the other night, he still holds a grudge against me for talking Nancy into breaking up with him."

"So, you're leaning toward him as a suspect? Is that it?"

Carley looked thoughtful. "I think we need to take a look at him. I do believe he could do anything if he got angry enough, even kill someone."

"Yeah, but the police need proof. I don't care much for Phil, myself, but that doesn't make him guilty of anything except being a jerk."

"I know, but I'm still going to talk to Russ about him. Even if Phil's not guilty, it won't hurt him to answer a few questions, will it?"

"No, I guess not, as long as we don't concentrate on him and forget to look for anyone else. It could be someone we've never thought of."

"I know that, but I want to get this man caught before he kills anyone else."

Yes, he knew what she wanted and understood why. She wanted this creep caught, wanted him in jail and for her and Kara to be safe from further threats. Well, both he and Nate wanted that too. But it wouldn't help any if the wrong guy got arrested. They couldn't jump to conclusions without some kind of proof. And so far, they had nothing.

The phone rang and Carley answered. Blake raised his eyebrows, questioning who it was. She mouthed, "Kurt."

Kurt Lister? Why was he calling her at home? Why was he calling her, period? He tried to remind himself it wasn't any of his business. He was leaving the country soon. What Carley did couldn't possibly concern him, and he knew he wasn't being sensible about this. He didn't want Kurt Lister or any other man calling her. So, okay, he was jealous. He didn't have a right to be, but that's the way it was.

She hung up and sat back down, shaking her head. "That was Kurt Lister."

"So I gathered. What did he want?"

"He just wanted to know if I was all right. He calls to check on me once in a while."

Blake noticed she sounded defensive. Probably she'd noticed he had a problem with Kurt. He didn't want him hanging around Carley.

She took a deep breath. "Where were we?"

"Trying to decide if we thought Phil Peterson was worth a second glance. I agree he is. But we have to keep an open mind. So far, we don't know enough about anyone to point fingers. Russ is a good cop, but we can't expect him to tell us what he finds out."

So was she interested in Kurt or not? He didn't really think Carley was the type to get involved with a married man. Maybe when she was younger, but she'd changed. He liked this Carley better, and he didn't want her thinking about anyone but him. And if that was being selfish, so be it.

"But he expects us to tell him what we learn."

"That's right. He's the police, we're not. So we play it his way."

She didn't reply to that. Not that he expected her to. He cared a lot for this woman, more than he should, and that streak of independence worried him. He liked it under normal circumstances, but this wasn't normal, and it could get her hurt, or worse. He'd do his best to keep an eye on her and keep her safe, but he was beginning to realize what a job that could be.

Blake left and Carley watched from the window as he drove away. The sudden surge of happiness she'd felt at seeing Blake had surprised her. Well, not really surprised her, but she hadn't expected to be this excited. Maybe it was because of all that had happened. Blake was the one person she felt she could depend on.

She had a hard time asking for help. Of course she had friends, but they weren't close enough for her to burden them with her problems. It was one thing to be grateful for anything that was done for her. It was something else again to ask people to do those things.

Blake hadn't supported her idea about Phil being guilty. Kara suspected the man Rachel had been dating. Maybe they were right. She might need to back off and slow down. Just because she didn't like Phil was no reason to jump to the conclusion he was guilty of murder. But she would still talk to Russ. It wouldn't hurt to check Phil out.

She also had an idea from the way he'd acted that Blake didn't like Kurt calling her at home. But why would he care? It wasn't like she was dating Kurt. She'd made some mistakes in her day, but dating a married man had never been one of them. Surely Blake wasn't jealous. If he was, that would mean he had feelings for her—feelings more than just a friend being protective of another. Sometimes, he acted as if he really cared for her, then he would withdraw, as if moving away emotionally. She kept hoping that would change. That he cared as much about her as she did for him.

She left the window to wander through the house. Sometimes, after all that happened, it felt more like a prison than a home. She stopped in her bedroom, staring at her reflection in the mirror. There had been a time when she had taken pride in her long, flowing blond hair and the gleam in her blue eyes, but she'd learned the hard way what was important. God, family, and friends were all that really mattered. She'd lost her parents, had lost Nancy, but she still had God.

She moved to the window, looking out. Yes, she had God, but she also had other friends, a church family, and Blake—for a while at least. He'd be leaving soon, and she didn't know what she'd do when he left. Somehow, she'd deal with it when the time came, the way she'd learned how to deal with everything she'd been through—by doing the best she could and trusting God. It had been hard to let go of her past—of the person she used to be—and at times, knowing that only God knew the answers was not easy to accept. But He had a plan for her, just like He had a plan for Nancy and for her parents. Her faith was all she had to rely on. She'd learned that the hard way after her parents died. The more she leaned on God, the more strength she had.

Somewhere out there, evil waited. Someone who had killed twice and who had his sights on her. And, entirely possible, on Kara? Whoever it was, he was determined not to leave anyone alive who was a threat to him.

He'd murdered two women. He wouldn't hesitate to kill two more.

Chapter Eleven

"Here you are. I thought you knew better than to mess around in my business." Carley, who had been bent over checking the bottom shelf in the dollar aisle of Brennan's Grocery, straightened so fast she had to grab the handle of her cart to steady herself. Phil Peterson stood in front of her, eyes cold and as hard as nails. Uh-oh. Russ must have talked to him about Nancy. She should have known this would happen.

She forced herself to look at him. "I have no idea what you mean."

"Oh no. Of course not. Like you didn't run to Russ, spreading lies about me. First you talk Nancy into dumping me, and now this. Keep stirring up trouble, and I'll teach you a lesson you'll never forget."

"You're threatening me? All I did was point out that both Nancy and Rachel were connected to you. If you're innocent, you don't have anything to worry about."

"You think I like having the police hauling me in for questioning? All because you can't keep your mouth shut. You're acting like a fool. People die every day. This one is no more important than the others."

She stared at him, shocked at the indifference in his voice. "But this is Nancy."

"And I'm supposed to care about a silly woman who threw me over for no reason except you didn't like me?"

He took a step toward her, and she shoved the cart between them. "Leave me alone, Phil. You mess with me, you're cruising for a bruising." Her father's words spewed from her mouth, catching her unawares. She could almost hear him saying that old cliché. That was just the way he had talked. She fought the memory. This wasn't the time to think of what she had lost. She needed to keep her wits about her.

Bob Tucker, the store manager, who had been a friend of Carley's parents and had tried to help her after their death, walked around the end of the aisle. "Everything okay, Carley?"

"I guess so, Bob. Phil was just leaving. Weren't you?" She stared at him while she spoke, and, unbelievably, he blinked first.

"Yeah. See you around."

He spoke directly to Carley, and she got the idea behind the words. He'd talk to her again. Probably when no one else was present, so he could get by without outside interference. He'd made his point—she still wasn't safe from him.

Phil left and Bob shook his head. "Watch yourself around that one. He won't do to mess with."

"I know. He's upset because Russ talked to him about the fact he knew both Rachel and Nancy." And Russ had that information because Carley had told him. And she wasn't sorry. The police needed to know about the connection between him and the two dead women.

"I see. I guess I'd forgotten that."

Carley looked up at him, surprised. "You knew he was trying to date Rachel?"

"It wasn't any secret. Phil gets mouthy when he's crossed. Particularly when it's a woman he's having trouble with. He has a hard time handling it. Know what I mean?"

"I know exactly what you mean. He has it in for me because I talked Nancy into walking away from him. Is he seeing anyone now?"

"No. I guess the women in Westfield have wised up to him. All except one. Seems to me I heard he got married a while back. Some woman quite a bit older than him. If I remember right, she's got money. Enough that Phil doesn't bother working anymore."

"That sounds like him. He wasn't much to work before, either."

"No more than he had to. I think they live somewhere out in the country. She must keep him on a short leash."

"I've seen him a couple of times lately."

"That so? Maybe he's getting tired of life down on the farm. He'd better not wander off too often, though. He wouldn't want his wife to get suspicious and kick him out. Poor guy might have to get a job."

A shopper stopped to ask him a question, and Carley smiled at him. "Well, I need to go. Thanks for stepping in to help me. I appreciate it."

"Anytime, and you be careful, girl. That guy's bad business. Stay away from him."

"I'll try." For all the good it would do her. From what she knew of Phil Peterson, she wouldn't have a choice. Bob was right about one thing. She did need to be careful. She guessed it could have been a mistake to talk to Russ—some people would probably think so—but on the other hand, if Phil had killed two innocent women, she wanted him caught. No matter what it took or what it cost her.

She paid for her groceries and pushed the cart out to her car. The lot was full and she kept glancing around, wondering if Phil was still there.

She thought about what Kara had said. The person they were searching for seemed to know where they were, where they were going, and who they had talked to. So which one would he be following today? A shiver ran through her at the thought.

She needed to tell Blake and Russ about the encounter with Phil. Blake had a right to know, and if she didn't tell Russ, he'd only become angrier about not having all the information. She understood why she needed to tell the chief, but she didn't want to tell Blake about the encounter.

Carley stared at her image in the rearview mirror, noting the frown she wore and the tight line of her lips. Why was it so hard for her to accept help from anyone? Particularly from Blake? She'd been this way all of her life, but she had been a little more accepting until Blake came along. What was it about him that made her fight him at every turn?

She knew the answer to that. She just didn't want to admit it. He scared her. Yes, she cared for him, more than she should, but getting too close to him would require commitment. What if she let Blake down the way she had everyone else she had cared about? She had been so immersed in the way he made her feel, she hadn't given a thought to long-term commitment. Could she handle that?

In spite of her doubts, she was strongly attracted to him. He made her feel safe, protected, and special. No matter how this developed, God had blessed her by bringing him into her life. She needed to calm down and let it all work out, one way or another.

When she reached home, she pulled out her cell phone and called Blake to tell him the latest development.

"He threatened you?" Blake felt his muscles tighten involuntarily. Phil Peterson had threatened Carley? The hand not holding the phone gripped into a fist. He knew just how Nate had felt. He'd like to get his hands on this guy. "Are you all right?"

"I'm fine. But doesn't that prove he has something to hide?"

Blake forced himself to calm down. He took a deep breath before answering. "Not necessarily. Phil's got a short fuse, and having Russ question him would be enough to send him over the edge. Phil's got a high opinion of himself. He thinks he's a cut above the rest of us."

"Especially above women. We're second-rate citizens to him."

Blake caught the bitterness in her voice and understood it completely. Phil hadn't been good to Nancy, and evidently, he'd acted the same way with Rachel. Maybe the guy did have something to hide. It wouldn't hurt to add him to their list of suspects. Their list of suspects? So far, that was a mighty short list.

"Look, Carley, I was just getting ready to go out and talk to people. You want to come along? I can't guarantee we'll learn anything, but at least we can try. What do you think?" And if she was with him, he could take care of her.

"I think that's a good idea. Better than just sitting around doing nothing. It's my turn to drive."

"Don't even think about it. This was my idea and I'm driving. I'll pick you up in a few minutes. Okay?"

He waited.

Finally, sounding a little irritated, her voice came over the line. "Okay, I guess. I'll be ready."

Blake hung up the phone, grinning. This was one independent woman, but he was going to wear her down. She needed him, and she might as well accept it because he was going to take care of her whether she wanted him to or not.

He parked in the driveway, and Carley came out of the house, locked the door, and hurried down the walk to the car. She must have been watching for him.

"So where are we going first?"

"I've got that list of people who knew Rachel. Of course it's not complete, but it's a place to start. First, we'll check out her neighborhood again. Okay?"

"Sure. Anything's fine with me."

When they reached the neighborhood where Rachel had lived, Blake parked the car. The first three doors they knocked on, no one answered. It was Saturday, so most people wouldn't be at work, but that didn't mean they had to be home. At the fourth house, a short, plump, white-haired woman answered the door.

Blake introduced himself and explained they were looking for information about Rachel. After a short hesitation, she invited them inside. Crocheted doilies decorated every table and each chair arm of the spotless house. A plain old tabby with white on its throat and a white ring around one leg lay on the back of the plush blue divan, staring at them. Drapes and sheer curtains hung at each window, and a grandfather clock stood in one corner of the living room. An old-fashioned braided rug lay in front of the divan, and pictures of people Carley assumed were family members were arranged on a long mahogany table.

The woman beamed at them. "I'm so glad someone is trying to find out the truth. I know the police are working on it, but I'd like to see everyone get involved. I'm Melba Curtis, and I just took a blackberry cobbler out of the oven. Would you like some?"

Blake's stomach said yes, but he forced himself to refuse. "We still have a few places to check out. Maybe some other time."

"In that case, let's sit down and get at it. What do you want to know?"

Blake settled into a comfortable, overstuffed blue armchair while Carley took an antique Boston rocker with a quilted cushion in the seat. "Anything you can tell us about her. First of all, did you ever see anyone you didn't know over at her house?"

Melba shook her head. "Rachel didn't have much company. Mostly she kept to herself. She was a sweet girl, though. Last winter when I had the flu, she brought me chicken soup and took me to the doctor. She was a good neighbor."

Blake thought about that. "So if she was seeing someone, why didn't anyone ever notice them together?"

Melba frowned. "You know the answer to that as well as I do. As pretty and sweet as Rachel was, any man who was free to be going out would have been proud to be seen with her. So look for a man who was already tied to someone. Not good enough for her, if you ask me."

"Yeah, we thought of that too. She doesn't seem like the type for something like that, though."

"She wasn't. But I suspect she was lonely. Rachel was quiet, not one to put herself forward. She didn't go out of her way to attract attention, but I think she would have enjoyed the chance to meet someone. Let some good-looking, no-account man make a play for her, and she could be swept right off her feet."

Blake nodded. So far, they weren't learning anything new, just the same thing everyone else thought. This scenario didn't seem to fit what they knew about Rachel Blevins. Everyone agreed she wasn't the type for something like this, so who had led her astray, if that was what had happened?

Melba was still talking. "It almost broke my heart when she stopped going to church. I knew something was wrong. But I firmly believe she would have come back to God someday. She was too strong, too committed to her beliefs to stay away forever. She'd have stopped seeing this man and come back where she belonged eventually."

She turned her head away from them, staring at the wall, looking so sad Carley could have cried for her. She didn't seem to have anything else to contribute, so after a moment of silence, Carley walked over to Melba and patted her shoulder. "I'm so sorry. I know it's hard."

Melba nodded but didn't say anything. Blake and Carley thanked her and walked out to the car. Carley got in and closed the door. "Who's next on your list?"

"What about someone she worked with?"

"Or her pastor."

Blake shook his head. "I've talked to him. He didn't have anything to contribute. Just that she suddenly stopped coming to church. He'd been to see her, talked to her, trying to find out if something was wrong, but she wouldn't tell him anything."

"So that sounds like she was hiding something."

"I think we've pretty well established that. There's a woman she worked with who lives here in town. Want to stop by and talk to her?"

"May as well, I guess."

Blake turned the car down another street. A few minutes later, they pulled up in front of a two-story, old-fashioned house with a wide front porch with a swing. A woman with dark hair and suspicious blue eyes stared at them.

"Yes?"

Blake explained what they wanted and waited. She hesitated and Carley stepped in, introducing herself and explaining why they were interested. She told the woman about Nancy's death and how it could be tied to the same person who had killed Rachel. "And now he's after me. Anything you tell us could save my life."

The woman's features softened and she gave one short nod. "All right. Come on in."

She stepped back to let them walk past her. "I'm Lora Milbank. I worked with Rachel, as I suppose you know, or you wouldn't be here."

"That's all we know," Blake said. "We appreciate you talking to us."

He guessed Lora would be in her early fifties. She was fairly tall, slim, and had a quick way of moving that seemed almost jerky at times. As if she was nervous. Well, maybe she had a right to be. Someone she knew had been killed, and she was talking to people she'd never seen before, and they were in her house. That could be enough to bring this creep down on her. Or maybe she wasn't sure about them. He couldn't blame her for that.

Lora's house wasn't as old-fashioned as Melba's had been. The brown leather couch and matching chair looked new. Crystal lamps graced the walnut end tables and the beige carpet was spotless. The only pictures were paintings—one of a sunset and one of a beach.

After they were seated, Carley leaned forward. "Did Rachel ever talk to you about someone she was seeing?"

Lora hesitated. "No, not really, but she started changing about a year ago. Rachel was friendly, upfront, always ready to listen. She didn't talk much, but people talked to her. I noticed she started holding back, not taking part in the breakroom gossip. I can't really explain it, but she was just different."

"How did she seem?" Carley asked. "Happy, disturbed, what?"

"That was the puzzling part. At first she seemed happy. You know, a spring in her step, light in her eyes, smiling all the time. After a few months, she began to gradually change. At the end, she just wasn't Rachel, if you know what I mean. She was quieter, not really focusing on anyone, like her thoughts were turned inward. I'm probably not explaining it very well, but it was like she was upset about something."

"Unhappy?" Carley suggested.

"Yes." Lora nodded. "Very unhappy. I was worried about her, but whatever was wrong, she wouldn't talk about it. If I asked, she just brushed me off. She was quiet and easily led, but she could be stubborn when she wanted to."

"Is there anyone she might have talked to, someone she was close friends with?" Blake asked.

"No. Oh, she had friends, lots of them. But like I said, she was a private person, not apt to talk about her life or her business. Mostly, she listened to others talk. You could have a visit with her and come away realizing she hadn't said much, that you'd done all the talking. She had a gift that way. People always talked to her."

"Did you ever see her with anyone?"

"I think I came close. I was in Dearborn's over in Oldham one day, looking for a new blouse, and I ran into Rachel. She seemed sort of flustered and cut me short when I tried to talk to her. I got a glimpse of her heading for the escalator and there was a man behind her. He was tall and dressed in jeans and a brown shirt. But his back was turned, and I didn't see enough to describe him or know him if I saw him again."

Carley sighed. "That's so frustrating. If only you had gotten a good look at him."

"I know. I thought of that after she was killed. If I could give the police a description, it might help catch her killer."

"Is there anything else you can tell us?" Blake asked. "Even if you don't think it's important, it might be something we could use."

Lora shook her head. "If I did, I'd tell you. I want this guy caught. Whatever Rachel was messed up in, she didn't deserve this."

Blake nodded at Carley, and she took a pen and pad of paper out of her purse and wrote down her phone numbers. "If you think of anything, would you call me? That's my home phone and my cell phone. Call anytime. I'm like you. I want this man caught."

They talked a few more minutes without learning anything and finally stood. "Thanks for talking to us, Lora." Blake shook her hand. "It was good to meet you."

"Good to meet you too. And if I learn anything, I'll be in touch."

They stepped outside and Lora shut the door behind them, but when they reached Blake's car, all four tires had been slashed.

Chapter Twelve

Carley sat at her home computer, searching for anything about Rachel Blevins. Blake had called Carson's Tire Company and had four new tires installed. Whoever was after her and Blake knew exactly where to find them. But how? They never told anyone where they were going, so how did he know so much about them? Just thinking about it made her blood run cold.

Carley turned her attention back to the monitor. She'd found Rachel's Facebook page, and from what Carley could see, she'd been a good person, but she hadn't posted anything very personal. She could understand Rachel wanting to keep to herself. She had learned the hard way that the less people knew about you, the better off you were. She moved out of the site and went to her email. Not that she was expecting anything. It was just a habit. She checked the thing a dozen times a day when she was home. Carley ran the cursor down the line of messages, stopping at one from No.1Badboy. She clicked on it and stared in disbelief at the words.

> YOU CAN RUN, BUT YOU CAN'T HIDE. YOU DON'T WANT TO MAKE ME MAD. I PLAY ROUGH.

Carley shoved her chair back as a quiver of fear snaked up her spine. Who was this and why was he hounding her this way? The silence overwhelmed her and she strained to hear. Nothing. The doors were locked. She'd made sure of that. She was safe here—or as safe as she could be, which didn't mean a lot anymore. Carley thought about that. No, she wasn't safe. She never would be until the person stalking her was caught.

The clamor of the phone shattered the stillness.

She hesitated, then reached for it. A harsh voice snarled over the line. "Are you thinking about me? I want you to, especially at night. I'm your worst nightmare." He laughed, then slammed down the receiver so hard it jarred Carley's eardrum.

She recoiled from the viciousness of the words. Who did she know who was capable of this type of behavior? But then, it didn't have to be someone she knew.

It could be anyone. She corrected that. Not just anyone. It had to be someone who had something to gain by harassing her this way. Someone who had killed twice and wouldn't hesitate to kill again. She sent the email message to Russ and mentioned the phone call. That was all she could do, and it probably wouldn't help much.

Carley glanced at her watch. She had ten minutes to reach the church to teach Wilda Hargis how to use the copier. The older woman had agreed to take over the bulletin but was a little nervous about the machine. Carley had volunteered to help the first time she had to use it. Would whoever was harassing her trail her to the church? She was so nervous that just the sight of a black SUV could throw her into a panic. She and Wilda would be alone at the church, so she'd have to make sure the doors were locked and her cell phone was handy.

Carley reached the church with a couple of minutes to spare. After she showed Wilda what to do and the bulletin was printing, the two of them chatted casually until the other woman cocked her head to one side, looking curious.

"How are you getting along with Sherman?"

"Sherman?" Taken by surprise, Carley couldn't think who she meant.

"Sherman Quigley."

"Oh, Mr. Quigley. Do you know him?"

"I went to high school with him, and he was something else. A girl in the neighborhood had a baby, and she said it was his. Took him to court. He had to pay child support. She moved away, and I don't know where she went or what happened to her or the baby. He'd be grown now."

Carley stared at her, stunned, although she didn't know why. Everyone had a past, and Mr. Quigley couldn't be an exception. He'd probably sown a few wild oats when he was younger. "You're talking about my boss?"

"That's right. Sherman Quigley. I guess he's calmed down a little now."

"I guess so."

"Well, he's older. Maybe he's learned to behave himself. He was a little wild growing up." The copier stopped running and Wilda got up to collect the bulletins. "Thanks for helping me, Carley. I don't think I'll have any trouble now."

"Well, if you do, call me. I'll be here if you need help."

"I appreciate that. I don't know what I'd do if I didn't have you."

Which was a far cry from the way Wilda had felt when Carley's parents had died. She'd been one of the church members who had blamed her for her part in it. They'd been right, of course, but she'd tried to change. Maybe she had succeeded a little. At least Wilda had come around to being friendly.

Carley left the church thinking of what Wilda had said before dismissing it. While it had surprised her, it was just gossip. What happened that long ago couldn't have any bearing on what was going on now.

When she returned to her car after stopping at the post office to buy some stamps, she found Phil Peterson leaning against her white Ford. Carley jerked to a stop, staring at him. Why couldn't he leave her alone? She glanced around and discovered she was on her own.

Phil had his arms folded as he relaxed against the door on the driver's side. His grin was nothing more than a malicious smirk, making it clear he thought she was at his mercy. Carly tilted her chin, forcing herself to stare back at him.

"Did you think you'd heard the last of me? No such luck."

"What do you want?"

"I just want to visit with you. I feel like I know you well. Real well. Nancy talked about you all the time."

Carley stared at him, stunned. Nancy wouldn't have betrayed her like that … would she?

"That's right. I know a lot about you. More than you want me to know. You were a wild one, weren't you? I'll bet people in this town would be shocked if they knew some of the things she told me."

Carly took a step toward him. "Get away from my car."

"Try and make me. You're going to pay for mouthing off to the police about me. No one treats me that way."

A new voice interrupted them. "Hey. What's going on here?"

Carley turned to see Kurt approaching.

"You got a problem?"

She nodded, glad to see him. Kurt could handle Phil. No problem. "You could say that."

Kurt moved closer, giving Phil a menacing look. "I don't know who you are, but if you're still here by the time I count to three, I'll rearrange your nose."

Phil straightened, all his bravado vanished. "Look. We were just talking."

"That's not what it looked like to me. Now get out of here while you still have time. I won't warn you again."

Phil licked his lips. "Okay. I'm leaving. No need to get riled."

He walked away and Carley turned to face Kurt. "Thank you. I really appreciate what you did."

"No problem. Glad I could help. What was his problem?"

"He's upset because I told the police he tried to date both Nancy and Rachel."

Kurt grinned. "I see. Well, maybe he has a reason to be worried. The cops are probably breathing down his neck, but if he's guilty, he deserves to be caught." He reached out to brush her hair off her forehead. "You okay?"

Carley nodded, not sure what to do. Fortunately, he'd solved the problem for her. He grinned and patted her shoulder. "Don't worry. I won't let anyone hurt you, but right now I've got to go. Marlene is waiting for me, and she doesn't like it if I'm late."

Carley watched him walk away, thinking her attitude toward Kurt was changing. She needed to stop jumping to conclusions about people. Kurt was a nice guy when you got to know him. He didn't put on airs. You just had to take him the way you found him. She decided Marlene Lister didn't appreciate what she had. It would be good to have a husband like Kurt taking care of you.

Carley drove home, still shaken by the episode. She needed to keep an eye out for Phil and try to avoid being alone with him. She'd learned something about him today. He wasn't just a bully—he was also a coward. He'd backed away from Kurt quick enough. But then most bullies were cowards. They usually picked on someone they didn't think could fight back. Well, she didn't intend to run. If he had anything to do with what happened to Nancy, she wanted him held accountable.

When she got home she called Russ and told him about her run-in with Phil. He assured her he would follow up on it. Later, Blake called to check on her.

"You doing okay?"

"I guess so."

"You don't seem very sure. What's going on, Carley? Talk to me."

"Oh, it's nothing much. Just a hateful phone call and an email message." She tried to sound calm, not let him sense the anger she really felt. She couldn't even relax in her own home without her enemy attacking her.

"So who called?"

"I don't know. He didn't give a name. The email was from someone who called himself No.1Badboy. I have no idea who that is. I guess he could be one of several people I know." She tried to keep it light, but her joke fell flat. Her nervous laugh had given her away.

"I'll drop by later. I want to see that email."

Carley thought about telling him she already had deleted it, but that would be a lie. Yes, she appreciated Blake's concern, but someone was going to get hurt before this was over and she didn't want it to be him. He'd be safer if he stayed away from her and stopped involving himself in this mess.

"Okay."

"See you later and be careful. I don't want anything to happen to you."

She didn't want anything to happen to him, either. Just thinking about it tore her apart. He ended the call and she bowed her head, asking God to take care of him. How could she bear it if Blake got hurt? Particularly if it happened because he was trying to protect her. Her parents, Nancy ... she'd lost so much.

Please, God. Not Blake. Please take care of him. She wondered if the police were making any headway in catching the killer. Russ hadn't told her anything, but then he probably wouldn't. He was the one trying to solve this case. She was the victim. A big difference there.

No, she didn't expect the police to tell her what they had learned, but Russ was avoiding her. Or, at least he wasn't going out of his way to talk to her. Maybe he didn't have anything he could share, but she felt as if he still blamed her in some way for Nancy's death. Or maybe something else was bothering him. She remembered the way he had treated her at the police station the night Nancy died. Add the fact that someone was keeping tabs on her comings and goings, and she wasn't as sure about Russ as she wanted to be.

But probably she was just jumping at shadows. After all, Russ was the law in Westfield. Maybe she should concentrate on Phil Peterson, who was a much more likely suspect. She should tell Blake about her run-in with Phil, but she needed to be careful with that. Blake didn't seem to like Kurt. As a matter of fact, Kurt didn't have anything good to say about Blake, but she couldn't see how that was her problem. And since Blake kept telling her he needed to know everything so he could help her, she really had no choice. She'd tell him, but she wasn't looking forward to it. So what was their problem anyway? They were both nice guys. Why couldn't they just get along?

Blake knocked on Carley's door and followed her to the screened porch. She gestured to the couch and chairs. "Let's sit out here. It's so nice out, I don't want to stay inside."

Blake settled into a wicker chair and glanced around. "This is great. Good place to sit and relax."

Carley probably found it hard to relax. Relaxing was difficult when your life was in danger and you had no idea who wanted to kill you. She was handling it well, but he realized she couldn't let her guard down, couldn't trust anyone. She could trust him and he hoped she knew it, but she needed to be leery of anyone else.

He leaned back and glanced over at her. "So. You had any more problems other than the phone call and the email?"

She hesitated and he shook his head. "Come on, Carley. Tell me what's going on."

"I had another run-in with Phil Peterson. I was at the post office and when I came out, he was leaning on my car and he wouldn't move."

"What did he want?"

"Oh, just the usual. He's upset because Russ questioned him, and is blaming me."

"Is that all?"

"Yes. Kurt came by just then and made him leave. I haven't heard any more from Phil. Maybe I won't."

"Kurt Lister? What was he doing there?"

"How would I know? I didn't ask him. I'm just glad he showed up when he did."

His eyes roamed her backyard before he decided to answer her. "Yeah, I guess that was good. Now show me that email."

"All right, but there isn't much to see." She led the way into the house and sat down at the computer. There were a few new messages, but she scrolled down and clicked on the one he wanted.

Blake leaned over her shoulder, reading. Anger flared through him as he concentrated on the words. The arrogance of this guy. He wanted her worrying about him? He played rough? Well, he wasn't the only one. Just let him get his hands on this creep, and Blake would teach him a lesson he wouldn't forget. And he would do all he could to help the police bring this guy down.

"Is this the only message you've had from him?"

Carley nodded. "Lately, anyway. I told you about the earlier one, but I'd just as soon not hear from him again."

"I think you need to tell Russ about the phone call and this email. He needs to know what's going on."

Carley swiveled around to face him. "I did tell him, but Blake, how sure are you that we can trust Russ?"

He stared at her, remembering his own thoughts about the policeman. But he was wrong. He had to be. Russ was his friend. He was the law in Westfield. Who could they trust if not him?

He pulled his thoughts together. "Do you have any reason not to trust him?"

After a moment, she shook her head. "No, nothing definite, but there's the way he acted at the police station, as if he was angry at me, like he thought it was my fault Nancy was dead."

"He explained that. The two of them were getting back together again and now it was ended. That's why he was upset."

"But were they really? Nancy was my best friend. She told me everything. If she and Russ had really been getting back together, why didn't she tell me?"

"Maybe she wasn't sure it would work. She might have wanted to wait, give it a chance before she talked."

Carley shook her head, and he could see from her expression she was growing more determined she was right. He needed to change the subject, get her talking about something else. Yes, he'd had some of the same thoughts, but they had to rely on Russ. He was all they had.

"Have you heard any more from Kara? Has she had any trouble lately?"

Carley looked shamefaced. "No. I should have called her. I promised to stay in touch. Do you think we should talk to her?"

"I think it might be a good idea. Why don't you call her?"

"Right now?"

He nodded, and she stood up and walked to the phone. In a short time, she was talking to Kara. Blake listened to Carley's side of the conversation. To his surprise, she promised Kara they would be right there. She hung up and he waited for her to speak. When she didn't, he prodded her. "Come on. What did she say?"

"She's had a phone call similar to mine, and her tires have been slashed too. I told her we'd be right over."

"Where's Nate?

"He's out of town on a job. Supposed to be back tonight. I think they're having some problems in their relationship. She said as much when she was here."

Blake remembered what Nate had said—that Kara was too strong in her beliefs to suit him. That was probably a good part of their problems. Nate lived a little on the wild side and Kara didn't. Unless that changed, he didn't see much chance of them resolving their differences. He waited until Carley grabbed her purse and then followed her outside.

When they reached Kara's, she was waiting for them. As soon as they were seated, Carley questioned, "You're getting phone calls too?"

"Yes. Threatening ones, like yours. He said I'd better keep my mouth shut about Rachel. He had connections and he knew everything I'd said to the police. If I kept talking, he'd have to stop me and I wouldn't like the way he did it."

Carley nodded. "He told me that he knew me and I didn't want to make him mad. That he played rough."

Kara took a deep breath. "What have we done to deserve this? He killed Rachel and Nancy, and now he's after us just because we were friends with them. That doesn't make sense."

"It does if you hold the key to identifying him," Blake said.

"But we don't. We have no idea who he is," Kara protested. "There's no way we could hurt him."

"But he thinks you can." Blake leaned forward. "This guy must have a lot at stake to take a chance like this, harassing two women who have done nothing to him." Of course, he was trying to avoid getting caught, but maybe there was more to it than that. Although it would be hard to think of anything more important than getting away with murder. Whoever was behind this persecution was really pushing it, which might work in their favor as long as no one else got hurt. If they were lucky, he'd mess up. Blake was beginning to believe that was the only way they could catch him.

Chapter Thirteen

Carley followed Mr. Quigley reluctantly after he called her into his office. What was he up to? She was working the reception desk and also spending part of her time with Juanita as an assistant, which she had a hunch was the first step to taking Nancy's job. Nothing she wanted to do, but she had decided to go along with him in an effort to discover what this was all about. If things got too dicey, she could always look for another job. This wasn't the only place to work, and she was too occupied with trying to learn who was harassing her to worry about Mr. Quigley and what he had in mind.

He waited until she sat down across the desk from him, then he leaned back in his chair, hands clasped across his stomach, looking totally relaxed. "I have a task for you. I'd send someone else, but there's no one I can spare right now. I'm thinking of merging with Barnes Manufacturing, and I want someone to take a look at their plant to see if they would be capable of producing our product. I want you to go over this morning and check it out."

Carley stared at him, bewildered. He wanted her to do what? She was a receptionist, an office worker. She knew next to nothing about the plant. Why would he choose to send her? This didn't make sense. The plant was full of people better qualified than she was for this job.

She cocked her head, giving him a skeptical look. "Why me? You must know I have no idea what you're looking for. Why not one of the plant supervisors?"

"Kurt doesn't want word to get out about what we have in mind. You'll pose as a newspaper reporter doing an article on the plant. He'll show you around and tell you what I need to know, and you'll report to me. I'd go myself, but that would give the game away. Don't worry, Carley. Kurt knows what I want, and he'll point out exactly what you need to look at."

So she was supposed to lie about who she represented and why she was at the plant. Every nerve she had was sending out a warning to say no, but this was her boss. She worked for him. Besides, while she really didn't want to do this, and there was also something off about it, it wouldn't hurt for her to see if she could learn anything. Not learn anything about the business, but find out what was going on with Mr. Quigley and the way he had been acting lately.

"All right, when do you want me to go?"

"This morning would be fine. Do you have GPS on your car?"

"Yes. Just give me the address and I'll get started. But first, I need a list of what I'm supposed to look for." He had to know she would be at a complete loss. She needed some idea of what she was supposed to find out.

"You won't need anything. Just take a notebook and pen with you, and Kurt will give you all the information. By the way, this is confidential at this point. I'd rather you didn't mention it to anyone else until it's a done deal."

A few minutes later Carley was in her car and headed for Barnes Manufacturing.

As soon as she was out of sight of the plant, she pulled into a parking lot and dug out her phone. She was still uneasy about all of this. In spite of what Mr. Quigley had said, she'd feel better if someone knew where she was going. She punched in Blake's number and listened to it ring. When he answered, she filled him in on what she was supposed to do.

He sounded puzzled. "You're going where to do what?"

"I'm going to Barnes Manufacturing, and Kurt is going to show me around the plant."

"Why you? Why not someone more connected to the work of the plant?"

"I questioned that, and he told me they didn't want it talked about until they had made the final plans. I'm supposed to be a reporter doing an article on Barnes. I'm just checking in to let you know where I'm going. I need to get started. I'll talk to you later."

Carley ended the call, thinking she shouldn't have bothered Blake. In spite of the way she felt about this, surely there wasn't anything wrong with Mr. Quigley's request. She knew Kurt and was beginning to like him. She'd be safe with him, whatever her boss had in mind. She just hoped she could avoid Marlene.

Forty-five minutes later she drove into the parking lot of Barnes Manufacturing. It was larger than Quigley's plant. Somehow, from talking to her employer, she had gotten the impression that it was smaller—that he was doing Barnes a favor by using them to produce his product. This plant would make two of his.

She went inside and asked for Kurt, but before he appeared she was confronted by Marlene. Her voice was stern and her eyes were cold, matching the hard line of her mouth. "You can talk to me. What do you want with my husband?"

Carley mentally stumbled, trying to come up with something to say. She was supposed to be a reporter, but surely Kurt's wife, the owner of Barnes

Manufacturing, would have some idea of the real reason she was here. She couldn't imagine anyone keeping secrets from her. Not if they wanted to merge with her plant.

Kurt walked around the corner, saving her from replying to Marlene's question. He smiled and held out his hand. "Good morning, Miss Sutherland. Good to see you." He turned to Marlene. "I forgot to mention the local paper was interested in doing an article about the plant. I thought it would be good advertising, and it's free. You can't beat that."

Marlene frowned. "Exactly what is this article supposed to be about?"

"Why, what a fine business it is and how it's such a blessing to the town. We hire a lot of people, and they spend that money locally. They're grateful for all we do, that's all. I promised I'd show their reporter around and give her enough information to write the article."

Marlene narrowed her eyes and frowned. "Have you worked out the details on the Bushmaster's account? We need to get started processing that order."

Kurt firmed his lips. "I'll take care of that as soon as I'm finished here."

"I have a better idea. You work on that contract, and I'll show Miss Sutherland around the plant. I could probably answer her questions better than you, anyway."

Kurt's face flushed brick red. Carley watched, fascinated, expecting him to explode into a tirade at his wife, but he snapped his lips shut and nodded before turning away and leaving her alone with Marlene.

While she stood, confused, wondering what to do next, Marlene gave one of her tight smiles. "Are you ready for your tour of the plant?"

Carley decided to go along with her. She'd come this far, she might as well go all the way, but did this woman have to be so rude? "Sure. You'll have to start from scratch with me. I don't know much about your company."

"I'll see that you learn. Just follow me."

Marlene turned toward the door and Carley fell in behind her, wondering what she was in for. Poor Kurt. That was no way for a wife to treat her husband, embarrassing him like that. She didn't deserve a man like Kurt Lister.

Throughout the tour of the meticulously clean plant, Marlene kept glancing around and then looking back at Carley, a haughty expression on her face and her lips flattened in a smirk. She seemed to take pride in displaying her business, pointing out details that didn't mean anything to Carley. She obediently jotted them down in her notebook, wondering how she was going to explain this to her boss. Then she decided she didn't care. If he wanted to know more about the plant, he could talk personally with Kurt. She still wasn't satisfied with what he had told her about this transaction.

They had been walking around looking and talking when Marlene stopped in front of an overhanging deck and turned to face her. "All right. Now suppose you tell me what this is really all about. You're not a reporter and I'm not a fool. Why are you really here?"

Carley stared at her, not sure what to say.

Marlene waited, eyes narrowed. "I remember you. We saw you in that restaurant with Blake Richards."

"Yes, and I remember you too." Remembered that she hadn't liked this woman, and her opinion hadn't changed on that. She had learned more about her during their half-hour stroll through the plant, and so far, she'd found nothing to like and quite a few things to not care for, particularly her rude behavior and the way she treated Kurt.

"As far as I'm concerned, this was just a farce to allow you to spend time with my husband."

Carley shook her head, denying the very idea. Maybe Marlene had a reason to be suspicious—Blake seemed to think so—but if you wanted your husband to stay faithful, maybe you needed to treat him decently.

"You must be delusional. If I wanted to spend time with someone, why would I pick a crowded, noisy, heavily populated place like this to meet? I find your remarks insulting, and I've had enough. I'll leave now. Thank you for showing me around."

She turned and walked away, Marlene's eyes stabbing her back as she followed Carley toward the plant exit. Carley stormed on ahead. If Mr. Quigley wanted any information about this place, he could get it himself.

A shout followed by a thunderous crash jarred her to her toes. She whirled toward the sound. A cloud of dust rising from the plant floor disappeared to show a large chunk of some sort of metal machinery lying in the exact spot where she and Marlene had stood only a moment before. Marlene was a short distance behind her, mouth open, eyes wide with fear.

Carley ran to her. "Are you all right?"

She swallowed, her face white and lips trembling. Finally, she nodded. "I'm okay. But if we hadn't moved, we'd both be dead by now."

Plant employees were rushing toward her. One man who seemed to be in charge reached them first. "What happened?"

Marlene turned to face him. "That's what I want to know. Why was that … that thing on the deck, and why did it fall?"

He shook his head. "I have no idea. It shouldn't have been up there in the first place. The only way to have gotten it up there was with the crane, and it's never in this part of the plant."

"You will report your findings to me before your shift is over. Do you understand me?"

"Yes, Mrs. Lister. I'll do that."

Marlene turned away from him to face Carley. "Luckily, we're both all right. Whatever happened, it had to have been an accident. I hope you understand that."

Carley understood all right. Marlene was probably thinking there might be a lawsuit. Well, she could put that notion to rest. Carley wasn't one of those people who always seemed to be looking for a reason to sue someone.

She shook her head. "As long as we're both all right, I don't see a problem."

Marlene stared at her for a couple of seconds, then nodded. "Fine. I'll walk you to the door."

They turned to find Kurt rushing toward them. "What happened? I heard a crash."

Marlene pointed to the group of people gathered around the piece of machinery. "That machine fell off the deck, barely missing both of us. Do you have any idea how it got up there?"

Kurt stared at her, shaking his head. "No, but I'm going to find out." He walked away, ignoring Carley.

Marlene watched him go, then turned and led the way out of the plant. Once outside, she took a deep breath. "That was a close call for both of us. I am so sorry it happened, and very thankful it wasn't worse."

Carley nodded. "Don't worry about it. We're okay. God took care of us."

"God?" Marlene seemed to be considering what she'd said. "Perhaps so. I'll have to think about that."

Carley walked to her car, noticing Marlene was still standing in the same spot, staring in her direction. She drove out of the lot and headed back to the office, wondering how Mr. Quigley would feel about Marlene pushing Kurt aside and conducting the tour of the plant herself. Well, she couldn't care less. And the next time he wanted to send someone on an errand like this, he could just find someone else or go himself.

She walked in the front door and made her way back to his office. Her boss was on the phone, but he shot her a surprised look and ended the call. "Back so soon?"

Carley nodded and sat down. "Things didn't exactly go as planned."

He frowned. "What do you mean?"

"In the first place, Mrs. Lister refused to let Kurt show me around. She took it on herself to do it instead."

"That woman! I hope you didn't tell her your real reason for being there."

"No, of course not, but something happened. A large piece of some kind of machinery fell off an upper deck, smashing into the floor where we had just been standing."

"An accident? Of course, it had to have been. Good thing neither one of you was hurt."

"A very good thing." A horrible way to die, crushed to death by a ton of metal. "In fact, I'm still very shaky. I think I'll take the rest of the day off. I'm just not up to working right now."

"Of course, of course. Go home and rest. That had to have been a bad experience. I'm sorry you had to go through it. Don't worry, I'll talk to Kurt later, just the two of us."

So why hadn't he done that in the first place? Carley thought about asking, but the aftermath of what she had escaped was beginning to hit. Exhaustion flooded through her, leaving her almost too tired to stand. She needed to get home, lie down, and work her way through this.

"Miss Sutherland, I'd rather you not tell anyone about this little incident. People may ask questions about why you were out there, and I'd prefer to keep it quiet for a little while."

Carley nodded without saying anything and walked out. Once home, she headed for the bedroom, flopping on the bed without even removing her shoes. She started to shake, a trembling rippling through her as the sound of metal hitting the floor resounded in her mind.

A very narrow escape indeed.

Blake had spent an unsatisfactory hour talking to Russ and trying to find out if they'd learned anything about who was after Carley. He understood why the police chief refused to reveal any details, but it still irked him. It wasn't like he wanted to know so he could gossip about it. He wanted to keep Carley safe, and he needed that information to know what or who to protect her from.

He was still concerned about her phone call this morning. She probably wasn't home, but he decided to drive by and check on things just the same. He parked behind her car and rang the doorbell, wondering why she was home so early. A few minutes passed before she opened the door. He took one look at her, the way she held on to the door frame, conflicting emotions flickering in her expression, and knew something was very wrong.

Blake pushed her gently out of the way and stepped inside. "What happened to you?"

She took a deep breath and shook her head.

He watched as she slumped into a chair and leaned back. Something had hit her hard, and he wasn't leaving until he found what was wrong. "Carley?"

She gave him a weak smile. "Give me a moment. I need to pull myself together."

Blake sat down and waited, burning with curiosity. He'd give her all the time she needed, but he intended to find out what was going on. Carley wasn't the kind to collapse like this. Something drastic must have happened to make her act this way.

He wanted to gather her into his arms and comfort her, but from the way she looked at him, he realized he had to listen first. Whatever this was, she needed to talk to him before she changed her mind.

She licked her lips and started talking. He listened, stunned, anger surging through him. He forced himself to calm down, to not disturb her any more than she already was. This wasn't the time to say what he really thought. Instead, he leaned forward, speaking quietly.

"Are you all right?"

She nodded. "I'm sorry. It didn't affect me much until after I reached the office. I came home and fell apart. It was close. Way too close. For Marlene as well as me."

"I can see that. I'm so glad you're both all right." This wasn't the time to tell her how glad he was. In fact, he wasn't sure he could put the way he felt into words. Some things just couldn't be expressed. They had to be shown. He stood and walked over to her, pulling her gently out of the chair. His arms closed around her, drawing her close to him as he murmured her name.

Carley leaned against him, and he could feel her body trembling. He rested his cheek against her hair, thanking God for keeping her safe. They stood that way for a couple of moments, then she drew back and looked at him. "Thank you. I needed someone to hold on to."

Someone? He wanted her to need him. Someone was generic. Anyone handy. That wasn't what he had expected. Didn't she know how much he cared for her? Blake released Carley and stepped back, not wanting her to see how her words had affected him. It was better this way. He wasn't in a position to get involved with her. His mind knew that, but his heart kept forgetting. He took another step back, putting a little more distance between them.

"Are you all right now?"

She nodded. "Better. Thank you."

Carley sat down and he followed suit. Blake thought of what she'd told him and realized he didn't trust Sherman Quigley. Actually, he hadn't trusted him before this had happened. After all, Nancy had worked for him. He couldn't see any connection between Quigley and Rachel Blevins, but if there was one, he'd find it. He was just thankful that Carley was safe, and if he had anything to do with it, she would quit her job with Quigley Enterprises immediately.

She looked at Blake, blinking back the wayward tears. "Marlene and I could have both been killed. The only thing that saved us was that I got upset with her and walked away, and she followed me. If it hadn't been for that, we'd both be dead."

"It sounds like God was watching over both of you. Was Marlene all right?"

"That's what I think too, and yes, she's all right. I can't understand why Mr. Quigley sent me out there in the first place. Nothing he said about it made sense."

It certainly didn't, and he was going to do a little snooping around on his own. It wouldn't hurt to learn a little more about Quigley either, and Blake was the man for the job.

Chapter Fourteen

After Blake left, Carley slumped down at her desk, not really wanting to turn on the computer, but knowing she needed to see if there were any new messages from the person who was determined to kill her or drive her crazy, whichever came first. What she really wanted to do was quit work and never go back to Quigley Enterprises again. She knew that was impossible, though. Something was going on and she needed to find out what, because for some reason, it seemed to involve her. At least by going to work she might have a chance to learn more about it.

Just what she didn't need—a second mystery. Mr. Quigley couldn't have anything to do with Nancy's or Rachel's death. Nancy had made it clear she didn't know the man in the restaurant. If it had been their boss, she would have said so. So where did Mr. Quigley fit in? Maybe she was mistaken, making a big fuss about nothing, but she didn't really think so.

The phone rang and she answered to find Kurt on the line. "Carley? I'm sorry about what happened. Are you all right?"

He sounded concerned, as if he really cared. "I'm fine. It was a close call, but I'm getting over it. How's Marlene?"

His voice hardened. "Pitching a fit, like always. For some reason, everything that goes wrong around here is my fault."

Carley didn't know how to answer that, so she didn't try. She had a hunch he was telling the truth. From what she'd seen and heard from Marlene, it was clear she must be a difficult person to live with.

"Carley? You there?"

"I'm here."

"Look, I shouldn't have said that. It's just that I'm still upset. I could have lost my wife and you. I just wanted to make sure you're all right and apologize for what happened. I'm really thankful no one got hurt."

So was she, considering she was one of the two women who would have been crushed beneath that heavy piece of machinery. "Yes, it was too close for comfort. Have you found out why the machinery fell?"

"Not yet, but as far as I can tell, it must have been too close to the edge. It's just a piece we didn't need right now, and someone stored it up there. Got it out of the way, but it sure wasn't a good place for it. It's a miracle you both weren't killed. I couldn't have lived with that."

Carley spared a thought to his wife and how overbearing and arrogant she was. How could a man like Kurt Lister live with that day after day and survive? He had to be a very special person to put up with the way she behaved.

"Well, I'll let you go, Carley. I just wanted to make sure you were all right."

"Kurt, why did Mr. Quigley send me out there? He could have talked to you on the phone and found out all he needed to know, couldn't he?"

"Well, yes, but that's Quigley. He wanted everything kept quiet, to make a big deal out of it. That's the way he is. I'm glad it fell through. He would probably have been a real pain to work with."

"Oh, it's all over? Why?"

"He went about it the wrong way. If he'd been upfront and approached Marlene in the first place, she'd have jumped at the idea. But after all that fuss about you being a reporter, she won't touch it. I tried to tell him it wouldn't work. She's too smart to fall for a dumb stunt like that, but you can't tell Quigley anything."

"So the tour wasn't your idea?"

"No, of course not. It was a bad idea from start to finish." Kurt paused, a heavy silence weighing over the phone. "Well, I'll talk to you later, Carley, and if you need anything, call me."

Carley hung up the phone more confused than ever. Why had Mr. Quigley insisted she take part in that charade? If she did what she wanted to do, she'd quit her job. Never go back. But even as she thought it, she knew she had to find out what was going on with him, because she believed he was up to something and it revolved around her. She wouldn't feel safe until she learned the truth.

Blake woke up, wondering why he would be worried about Carley. The feeling that something was wrong haunted him. He glanced at his watch. One thirty. Too late to call her, and besides, what would he say? *I just called to see if you were okay?* At this hour of the night?

Still … it wouldn't hurt to drive by, just check things out, see for himself nothing was wrong. He reached for the pair of jeans he'd tossed over a chair and started to get dressed. Socks, shoes, and the navy blue sweatshirt he'd worn yesterday. He grabbed his car keys off the dresser and crept through the house, stepping lightly so he would not wake his mother.

The sky was overcast, and the air, cool and crisp, with a light breeze, smelled like rain. He drove to the right street, going around the block so he'd pass on the side closest to Carley's house. As he approached, he could see the windows were dark. She was sleeping, no doubt. Just what he should be doing instead of driving around in the middle of the night because of a feeling.

Wait a minute!

Was that a black SUV? Blake drove closer, trying to get a look at the license plate. That vehicle had been slowing as if turning into Carley's driveway. It speeded up. Blake hit the gas, trying to get closer. The SUV's lights came on. Because he was planning to break into her house. He wouldn't want his lights to give him away.

Blake's headlights picked up the SUV's license plate, but a big blob of dried mud covered what should have been a Missouri license tag. The other driver put on a burst of speed, running a stop sign. A car passed in front of Blake, bringing him to a screeching stop. The SUV's tail lights disappeared around a curve. Blake slapped the steering wheel, frustrated. Of all the luck. He'd have caught the guy if those two cars hadn't been in the way.

He drove back past Carley's house, ascertained all was undisturbed, then he headed toward the police station. Not that he had much to tell, but he'd let Russ know what he'd seen.

The police station was quiet. Russ was in his office, going over a stack of paperwork. He looked up when Blake walked in. "What brings you down here in the middle of the night? Anything wrong?"

Blake settled into the chair across the desk from Russ. "I think there may be."

"Yeah? What?"

"I drove past Carley's house tonight and a black SUV was in front of me. The guy slowed down and looked like he was intending to turn into her driveway. He sped up and turned his lights on when I pulled in behind him."

"Was she still up?"

"No, the house was dark and all her lights were out."

"So a black SUV with its lights off, just the kind of car we're looking for, was turning into Carley's driveway when she was asleep. Yeah, that does smell like something wrong. What were you doing driving past there as late as it is?"

"I woke up worried about her. It bothered me so much I decided I'd drive by and check it out."

"May be a good thing you did."

"That's what I'm thinking. It looked like most of the neighbors were down for the night too. Not many lights anywhere."

"And this guy just decided to visit Carley. I'm betting he wouldn't have rung the doorbell either."

"I think she's in danger. He's really after her. What can I do to help?"

Russ shook his head. "Nothing. This is a job for the police."

"Look. I can't just sit back and wait for someone to get to her. You know that."

Russ' expression gentled. "Yeah, I know. It's tough. I can't stop thinking about Nancy, wishing I'd been there for her. It's hard to deal with."

"Then you must understand how I feel about this. How could I live with myself if something happened to her and I didn't do anything to stop it?"

"I do understand, but I can't let a civilian get involved in an investigation. You have to accept that."

"You can't stop me from driving by her house a few times a night. That's surely not against the law."

"No, I guess I can't stop you from doing that, but you be careful and don't let the way you feel about Carley cause you to break the law. If you see anything, you call us."

"What if there isn't time?"

"You call. This is a small town; we can be there in a few seconds. I mean what I say, Blake. I realize how important this is to you, but don't tackle this guy by yourself. You call, we'll come."

"I'll keep it in mind."

Russ shook his head. "Don't just think about it. Do it."

Blake left the station and headed home. He had a lot to think about—Carley's safety came first. But something Russ had said stuck in his mind. It sounded like the police chief thought he was overly connected to Carley. He was strongly attracted to her, worried about her, devoted his time to taking care of her as much as he could. But love? Yeah, if he was honest, he just might be headed that way.

At work the next morning, Mr. Quigley stopped by Carley's desk and asked how she was doing. "All right. Since neither one of us was hurt, I guess there's no point in making a big deal out of it."

A misleading statement because she didn't mean a word of it. It was a very big deal to her. She wondered how Marlene was holding up. Was she back at work today, walking through the plant? Probably so. She was a strong woman. An arrogant, overbearing woman, but strong.

Things went well at work, but Carley was glad when it was time to go home. She was still thinking about looking for a different job but was wavering between wanting to get out and suspecting something was going on at Quigley Enterprises. Something told her that she needed to stick around and learn more about it and how it affected her. She'd talk it over with Blake, but she knew in advance what his opinion would be.

She hadn't been home very long before the phone rang. Carley smiled and shook her head at Blake's call. He was checking to see if she was all right. "Yes, I'm fine. What did you do today?"

"That's the other reason I called. I hope you won't be upset with me, but I told Russ about what happened at the Barnes plant."

"You did what? Why did you do that? It was an accident."

"How do you know that?"

"Well, what else could it be? Was that all you told him?"

"I also told him how Quigley acted. I still think there was something fishy about him sending you out there."

Well, so did she, but she wasn't sure she wanted Russ snooping around, asking questions. "Listen, Blake. Mr. Quigley doesn't have any reason to harm me. He tried to use me for his own purpose, but I'm not sure what it was. And yes, I'm concerned about it, and I don't trust him, but how could he cause an accident out at the Barnes plant when he wasn't even there?"

Blake was silent for a minute, and she wondered if he was still on the line. "Blake?"

"I'm here. I'm thinking about it. I agree he didn't have anything to do with Nancy's death, and he wasn't out at Barnes, but something about him just doesn't sit well with me. I'd feel better if you worked someplace else."

So would she. In fact, she had halfway planned to give notice today, but everything had gone smoothly and her boss had barely acknowledged her presence. Still, as far as she was concerned, her days at Quigley Enterprises were numbered. She'd swung back and forth on this issue for too long.

"Carley?"

"I know, and I'm thinking about it, but I can't quit until I have something else lined up, and jobs aren't all that plentiful here."

"I guess that's right, but I'd feel more comfortable about it if you were out of there."

Carley stared out the window. She didn't want to talk about this. "Have you learned anything new about the investigation into Nancy's death?"

"No. Whatever Russ knows, he isn't going to share it with me. But I haven't been able to find out anything on my own. I'm still trying, though, and so is Nate."

"Nate?"

"Yeah, he's an all-right guy when you get to know him, and he's determined to find out who's threatening Kara. I feel sorry for this jerk if Nate catches up with him. He'll be begging for the police. I have a hunch Nate plays rough."

Carley caught her breath. That's what the person who'd called her said about himself. That couldn't have been Nate, could it? No, of course not. They hadn't even learned about Kara being a friend of Rachel's when she got her first call. She didn't like how this situation was making her distrust everyone.

"You might be right. I want to trust him, and Kara needs someone on her side. But I don't think it would be smart to cross him."

"No, not a good idea at all. Call if you need anything, Carley. You know I'm here for you."

She thanked him and they hung up. Nate wasn't her type of man. She preferred someone a little more dependable, a little conservative in his dress and lifestyle. Someone like Blake. A few moments later, Carley wandered into the kitchen and checked the back door. She knew both doors were locked, but she still felt compelled to check. She peered out the glass in the back door, her eyes scanning the yard, but nothing seemed out of place. The living room was neat, only a half-read magazine lying on the dark green divan. The pinch-pleat drapes—green to match the divan—were closed, keeping anyone from looking in. After turning on both night lights, she switched off the lamps and entered her bedroom. The Irish cream drapes—off-white with a silky finish—beautifully contrasted her medium blue bedspread and darker blue carpet. This was her refuge. She could lie in bed, reading her Bible, and talk to God. This was the most peaceful place in her world.

After getting ready for bed, she turned out her bedside light and walked over to the window, pushing the curtain a few inches away from the frame and peering out. Nothing. No one driving down the street. No one walking past. Everything was peaceful, silent. Too silent?

She liked it peaceful and quiet, but for some reason, the stillness seemed to overwhelm her, heavy, stifling, smothering. She turned away from the window and walked back to the bed.

Carley tossed and turned for a good hour before getting up and going to stand at the window again, looking out. Someone out there wanted to kill her. She hadn't done anything to deserve this sort of treatment, and she was tired of putting up with it.

She paused, considering. Or had she? Was God punishing her because of her parents' death?

But God didn't work that way, did He? The relationship she had found with Him after her parents' death had been the only thing that kept her going. Although she knew it was time to move on, she still lived with it, with the guilt she could never quite escape. Carley's past may be behind her, but it was part of who she had become. Maybe, with God's help, she could be free at last. At any rate, God was the most important thing she had going for her.

A car drove by slowly, as if the driver was searching for something. A car she recognized. Blake. Why would he be driving past here this time of night? Creeping by, actually. There was only one reason she could think of. He was trying to make sure she was safe.

Carley heaved a sigh. That was so sweet of him but entirely uncalled for. He needed his rest, and she didn't want Blake to come upon the killer and get hurt or worse. How could she handle something like that? She had too much to feel guilty about without adding more.

Carley turned from the window and went back to bed, hoping she could get some sleep. She snuggled deeper into the bed, closing her eyes. Maybe if she lay still, did some deep breathing, sleep would come.

The next morning, after a quick breakfast, she dressed comfortably in beige pants and a turquoise sweater and drove downtown. No matter what happened, life went on. Bills had to be paid and she had to eat, although she couldn't forget that someone was just waiting in the shadows, wanting to get rid of her.

She filled the car with gas and then parked across from The Guiding Light bookstore, planning to pick up a newspaper and look at the help wanted ads. She'd looked online but hadn't found anything she was interested in, so the local paper was her next choice for options.

Traffic was heavy, so she walked to the end of the block to the closest stop light, which turned red as she approached. There were several people standing with her: three men, a man and woman with a young boy, and some women about her age who were laughing and talking. Carley shifted from one foot to the other, glancing around nervously. Maybe it was the aftereffects of the accident at Barnes Manufacturing, but she didn't feel completely comfortable anywhere.

Someone bumped against her and jerked her purse out of her hand, almost throwing her off balance. A man standing close by caught her arm, steadying her. She whirled, looking for the culprit. A red-haired boy, looking maybe thirteen, darted through the group of pedestrians, carrying her purse, an oversized monstrosity of black, gold, and green print with an elaborate gold-studded clasp.

"My purse! He stole it!" She pointed at him, trying to push her way past people to charge after him.

A bulky, somewhat overweight man, stomach hanging over his waistband and bald head shining in the sun, grabbed the boy, holding him.

Carley pushed toward them, plunging through the crowd. "My purse! Why would you steal it?"

The boy blinked at her, looking scared. "It's not my fault! That guy paid me to take it."

Carley swerved around, staring at the surrounding crowd. "Who paid you?"

"Him." The boy glanced over his shoulder. "He's gone."

"Probably wasn't no one there to start with," the man growled, pulling Carley's purse away from the boy. "You're just trying to blame someone else because you got caught."

"No! There really was someone. I'm not taking all the blame for this. Let me go!" The boy swung around, kicked the man's leg, jerked away, and ran across the street, forcing the driver of a blue Chevy to slam on his brakes and yell at him.

"Ow!" The heavyset man grimaced in pain.

"Are you all right?" Carley cried as she reached for him.

"Little brat kicked me." He handed her the purse and bent over to rub his leg. "I'd like to get my hands on him. I'd teach him a thing or two." He straightened and gave her a crooked grin. "At least you got your bag back. Kinda big, isn't it?"

"Way too big." But stylish, which was why she had bought it. That and the fact that Nancy had insisted it was perfect for her. She really wasn't all that crazy about it. And it was the same one she had been carrying the night Nancy was killed. Maybe she needed to get rid of it, get rid of the memories, if that was possible.

He looked down at her. "Are you okay? He didn't kick you or anything, did he?"

"No, I'm all right, but I appreciate you getting my purse back for me. It's got a lot of my personal information in it."

"Yeah. We carry around too much stuff that could cause problems for us if it got in the wrong hands. Not too smart, I guess."

"But necessary in today's world." She thanked the man and watched him limp down the street before making her way back to the car. The boy had disappeared. Why had someone paid him to steal her purse? She suspected the boy had been lying because he had gotten caught. Trying to shift the blame.

It didn't matter. Whatever the truth was, she had her purse back but she had lost all desire to shop. All she wanted to do was go home, get off the streets, and lock herself inside … where she should be safe but really wasn't. No place was safe for her anymore.

Blake drove past Carley's house at nine o'clock. It was his second time that night, and he planned to make the trip at least two or three more times. There was a light in what he remembered to be Carley's bedroom, so he guessed she was getting ready to turn in. Kind of early, but she'd been through a lot lately. He thanked God again that she was safe. That accident at the Barnes plant could have been really bad—if it *was* an accident. It seemed strange to him that a heavy piece of machinery would be stored on an overhead deck. Not a good idea. Whoever did it should have known it would be dangerous.

Blake turned at the corner and drove back home. He'd suggested to Russ that he have a policeman drive past Carley's house occasionally and make sure everything was all right, but Russ had vetoed the idea. He'd claimed he didn't have enough men to take on the job. Blake wasn't sure if that was the truth, but whether Russ approved or not, he would check on Carley as often as he pleased.

And Monday morning he was going to follow her to work. If she knew, she'd pitch a fit, but her safety was worth it.

Sunday morning, Blake walked into the kitchen, where his mother was busy icing a cake before going to church. Comfortably plump, wearing an old pair of brown slacks and a yellow cotton shirt, the rumpled condition of her salt-and-pepper hair showed she'd only given it a hasty combing. She glanced up at him, her eyes holding a question. "Did I hear you talking to Carley the other day about Sherman Quigley?"

Blake hesitated. He hadn't told her much about Carley's situation because she had a tendency to get involved without thinking about the consequences. He didn't want to put her in danger too. She looked at him, her eyebrows raised and lips firmed—the "look" she used to give him and his sister when they messed up.

After thinking about it, he decided to tell her about what had happened at Barnes Manufacturing. By the time he finished, her eyes were glittering with anger. "He sent her over there, pretending she was a reporter? That doesn't even make sense, and I'll bet Marlene wasn't fooled one bit. She'd never fall for anything like that."

"I gather she wasn't supposed to talk to Marlene. She was supposed to talk to Kurt but Marlene took over."

"That sounds like Marlene. That woman grew up thinking she was something special because her daddy was a senator. Her mother isn't much better. I always wondered why Marlene married Kurt. He was just a salesman in the plant, definitely beneath what she would feel was worthy of her."

She added a dollop of icing to the cake and spread it around. "There now. Don't I sound like an old gossip? But truth's truth, no matter how you slice it."

"What about Quigley? Is he from around here?"

"He grew up here, but he and his folks moved away after he graduated from high school. I'm not sure exactly where they went, but a few years ago Sherman moved back here and opened Quigley Enterprises. I think he's done fairly well—hires several people, anyway—but his plant isn't anything at all like Marlene's business."

After lunch, he called Carley, and when she answered he quickly got to the point. "Want to ride out to Walnut Lane subdivision with me? Nate got a lead on someone who might know something about Rachel. A woman she hauled around, shopped for, took to the doctor, that kind of stuff. Russ probably talked to her, but if he did, he won't tell us anything."

"All right. When are we going?"

"How about right now? I'll drop by your house and pick you up."

"I'll be ready."

Carley hung up the receiver, and Blake relaxed. If he had her with him, he would know she was all right. He could keep an eye on her and do his best to take care of her. Carley's expression was solemn, and on occasion her eyes appeared vacant, void of life and light. He could tell all of this was getting to her. This person had taken away her freedom, and he controlled what would happen next in her life. No wonder she had lost that air of confidence she used to wear. She had no idea what would happen next. Maybe this woman would have some information that would help them.

Blake picked her up later and as soon as she got in the car, she started talking. "How did you find out about this woman?"

"Nate has been poking around in Rachel's past. Seems she's someone Rachel knew from church and the woman needed help. Rachel volunteered and had been looking after her for several months. I'm thinking Rachel may have talked to her about this guy. Won't hurt to ask, anyway."

"No, probably not."

He knew this could very well be another dry run. What were the chances this woman knew anything? At least they needed to see her, check it out. Maybe it would be a dead end, or God could be smiling on them, giving them a lead that would pan out.

Blake turned into one of the older subdivisions and stopped in the driveway of a one-story white house with gray shutters. The lawn was neat and well cared for but without any flowers or shrubs—a stark contrast to the rest of the houses on this block, which all had decorative landscaping, some of them with concrete figurines or animals mixed in with the plants. "I guess this is it."

He rang the doorbell, and after a wait of several minutes, a short, thin woman balancing herself on a walker opened the door. Dropped shoulders brought her bowed head, covered in short, snow-white hair, to Blake's midsection and indicated the woman's exhaustion and pain.

She stared at them for a second before speaking. "Yes?"

"Mrs. Burton?"

She nodded. "Who are you?"

He introduced them and said that they were investigating Rachel's death. Tears filled her eyes as she motioned for them to come in. Mrs. Burton shuffled to a brown leather recliner and sat down. Carley took a seat on the copper-brown stuffed sofa. Blake chose the burgundy chair.

He glanced at Carley and started talking. "I understand Rachel helped you a lot."

The older woman's voice quivered. "She did everything and wouldn't take a cent for it. I don't know what I'll do without her."

Carley tilted her head, eyes charged with sympathy. "Don't you have anyone to help you?"

"Not really. The health nurse comes by once a week, and once in a while my niece will call, but for the most part, I'm on my own."

"I see." Blake made a mental note to see this woman had the help she needed. He'd talk to the pastor at church and see what they could do. If nothing else, he'd take care of it himself as long as he was there. His mother would take over when he had to leave. Martha Richards enjoyed helping others.

"Rachel was the most loving, giving person I ever met. She believed in God, and she lived her beliefs." Mrs. Burton wiped her eyes. "It's a shame more people aren't like her."

"And yet someone killed her," Blake pointed out.

"And I know who."

Blake shot her a startled glance. "You know who did it? Who?"

"I don't know his name, but she met him last year. At first they met for lunch, always out of town, which should have been a tip-off for her. But Rachel ... well, she was sort of inexperienced about life. Church and her work were the most important things for her. Then it became shopping, movies, dinner, and always somewhere away from Westfield."

"From what I've heard, she wasn't the type for that kind of relationship," Carley commented.

"She wasn't. But I think she was lonely. I believe this man paid a lot of attention to her, getting her involved with him. Someone who thought he could do anything he wanted and get away with it. But I also believe he may have had a lot to lose if the wrong person found out about it."

"Then why would he start a relationship with her if it could cause him trouble?"

Mrs. Burton shook her head. "Some people are that way, liking to take chances, sure they'll never get caught or have to pay. Most of them end up getting caught, but they never believe it could happen to them."

Blake nodded in agreement. "And you think what?"

She sat silent for a moment, then took a deep breath. "I think he was pressuring her to go farther than she wanted to. Rachel ... well, she had morals. She wouldn't have been quick to get involved that way with a man. She'd have wanted to get married."

Blake nodded. "That's what I think too. Rachel was pushing him to marry her, and he killed her to keep her from messing up his playhouse. He had a wife at home who wouldn't take that very well."

"So he got rid of her." Mrs. Burton's dark eyes snapped with fire. "He killed a decent woman who wouldn't do anything to hurt anyone. Rachel wasn't as cautious about people as she could be. I think it was the way she was brought up. She was inclined to look for the good in everyone. She met someone who took advantage of her and then got rid of her."

Yeah, that's what Blake thought too. Rachel turned her back on those values she lived with and got herself in trouble with a no-good jerk who killed her before she could cause him problems. And he was after Carley and Kara because he was afraid they might know something about him. Somehow, he had to be stopped.

Mrs. Burton shook her finger at Blake. "I'll tell you one thing. God won't let him get away with this. He'll get what's coming to him, sooner or later, and I hope I'm alive to see it."

Chapter Fifteen

Carley threw back the blanket and sat up, unable to sleep. Frustrated, she wandered through the house, stopping at the front bedroom window, thinking of Blake. They hadn't even dated yet, but they were linked together with a strong bond. Part of it was their shared faith, but there was more. He was becoming an important—a natural—part of her life. He'd be deploying soon, and she didn't know what she'd do when he left. She didn't want to think about it. She'd never felt this way about anyone else. She'd dated several men and she'd always enjoyed being with them, but this was deeper, more meaningful … more real than all of those combined.

Being with Blake felt right, like they belonged together. She knew his every expression, the way his eyes brightened when she walked into a room. The warmth of his hand in hers, the way her heart beat faster when he was near. He'd been so good with Mrs. Burton, the elderly woman they'd recently visited, but then he was good to everyone, especially her. He was so comforting, so strong, so determined to keep her safe. But her feelings were much more than just feeling thankful for him. She hesitated to admit it, but she was in love with him, the kind of forever love between the right man and the right woman. It would destroy her if anything happened to him.

She stared at the street outside. Overhead, stars pinned the darkness of night to the sky covering her silent neighborhood. Carley stiffened as a black SUV drove into sight, slowing in front of her house. She stepped back, not wanting to be seen, but it was too late. The glow of the light in the hall revealed her shadow against the windowpane. The car lights flicked from dim to bright and then back again several times, as if the driver was taunting her. Then it resumed speed and drove out of sight.

Carley took a deep breath and moved away from the window to slump down on her bed. She was sure the driver of that car was the same man who was harassing her. It was the same kind of car, and who else would be driving past her house, flashing his lights at the slightest hint she might be watching? He wouldn't stop until he had succeeded in getting to her, and it was beginning

Hidden Danger

to look like there was no way to stop him. Finally, she turned out the light and crawled into bed, but sleep was a long time coming.

The shrill screech of an alarm going off jolted her awake. She jerked upright in bed, coughing as smoke clogged her throat. Her heart pounded so loudly in her ears, it was like someone beating a drum.

Smoke?

She tumbled out of bed, pulling on her robe as she wound her way through her bedroom. Smoke swirled around her and flames hissed their way up the walls. Carley dropped down to avoid the smoke and crawled into the living room, bumping her shoulder on the coffee table hard enough to raise a lump. Reacting without thinking, she automatically grabbed her purse from the small table by the door. Panic-stricken, Carley fumbled with the lock on her front door, turned it, then jerked the door open and stumbled outside, gagging and coughing. A scream of sirens split the night. John Tolbert, her next-door neighbor, ran toward her.

"Carley? Are you all right?"

"Yes … no … my house…" She fumbled for her phone, grateful she'd had enough sense to bring it with her. "I have to call someone."

John patted her shoulder. "Don't bother. I did that as soon as I saw the flames. The fire department is almost here."

Carley sagged and he caught her, holding her for a moment before stepping back.

"Neta is here. She'll take care of you."

He released her and his wife took over, hugging Carley and patting her back. "You're safe. That's what really matters."

Carley fought back tears. Yes, she was all right, but her house wasn't. Her home. Flames shot above the roof at the back of the house. She gripped Neta's hand, too overwhelmed to speak. The fire trucks arrived with sirens screaming. Men tumbled to the ground and surged into action, directing a stream of water toward the flames. Neighbors poured from their houses, running toward them as Carley stood in the wet grass, watching her house burn.

Why, God? Why is this happening to me? She demanded silently. *Help me, please help me.*

But the house kept on burning.

Blake woke to the sound of sirens drawing closer. He threw back the covers and hurried to the window. Flames a few blocks over filled the sky. Carley's house! He was sure of it. He struggled into his clothes, buttoning his shirt as his mother rushed into his room.

"Blake! There's a fire and it looks like it might be close to Carley's house, or maybe it's hers."

He noticed she was already dressed. Grabbing his car keys, he moved toward her. "I'm going to check it out. I'll let you know what's going on."

"Forget that. I'm going with you." She whirled and ran toward the front door and he followed, knowing it would be useless to try to stop her. They hurried to his car and got in, and he whirled out of the driveway, going much too fast. All he could think of was Carley. She'd be all right. She had to be.

But fear left a bitter taste in his mouth.

Blake parked as close as he could get, and his mother was out of the car before he got the motor shut off. She rushed through the crowd, head turning from side to side as she looked for Carley. He spied her standing off to one side with Neta Tolbert. His mother made her way toward them and he followed, wanting to hold Carley, comfort her, assure himself she was all right.

His mother grabbed Carley, holding her so tight Blake saw her wince. "You're safe. I was so worried."

Carley wrapped both arms around her. "Oh, Martha. I don't know what happened. I woke up and the house was on fire."

Blake caught them both in his embrace. "Thank God you're safe."

Yes, thank God. Thank Him for saving Carley. He buried his face in her hair, smelling the fragrance of her perfume mixed with the stench of smoke. She could have died so easily in that burning house. But for the grace of God, he could have lost her that fast.

Flames licked higher. The firemen struggled to quench them, but a breeze kicked up, defeating their efforts. Another truck arrived and drove through her front yard to the rear of the property, where the flames were the strongest, attacking the fire from that direction. Gradually, the flames burned lower.

Blake kept his arms around both women, wishing he could do more. They stood that way for what seemed like a long time but probably wasn't. Eventually, his mother pulled away, and after a slight hesitation, so did Carley. His arms felt cold and empty. Some women from church arrived and he backed off, feeling in the way. He moved toward the fire truck, wondering about the damage to Carley's house. It looked like the firemen would be able to save part of the house. Probably not much of it, though, and everything that didn't burn would be smoke-damaged.

He stood there, just watching, knowing there was nothing he could do.

A couple of women who had been standing a short distance away turned and walked past so closely he couldn't help overhearing their conversation.

The dark-haired one stopped to look back at the house. "Poor Carley. She's had a hard life. It seems like nothing goes right for her."

The second one, an older woman with a mop of gray hair, snorted. "Don't expect me to feel sorry for her. She killed her parents, you know. Payday's been a long time coming. It's way overdue."

The women moved away, leaving Blake to stare after them. She killed her parents? He'd heard they died in a car wreck, and even that Carley was driving, but there seemed to be more behind the hateful voice of the older woman. Was that what people thought of Carley? No wonder she looked so vulnerable sometimes, so lost.

The flames were down to coals, but the firemen were still working with them. The stiff breeze whipped the remaining fire, sending sparks flying. Blake made his way to where his mother and Carley were standing. People were starting to move off, leaving slowly. Neighbors were standing on their porches, evidently reluctant to go inside.

His mother turned to face him. "I've convinced Carley to come home with us. No use in her going to a motel at this late hour."

He hurried to support her. "That's right. We've got an extra bedroom, and you need to get some rest. This has been a rough night."

Her expression crumpled and he thought she would dissolve into tears, but she pulled herself together and gave them a wavering smile. "I appreciate it so much. It will be good to get away from here."

"Then let's go," Blake said. "There's nothing to gain by standing around. We'll come back in the morning and check out the damage and see what we can salvage, but you can't do anything tonight."

She nodded, but before they could turn to go, Russ walked toward them. "Hey, Carley. I'm sorry about this, but at least you got out safe and sound. That's something to be thankful for."

"Do you know how it started? It looks like it's at the back of the house where I was sleeping."

Russ looked like he wished he were somewhere else. "Yeah, it started there. I talked to the fire chief. He says it looks like arson."

Arson? The air rushed out of Blake, as if someone had punched him in the stomach. Someone had set the fire? He stopped to consider the idea. Well, yeah, why not? Someone was trying to kill her, and he'd just upped the ante.

"Arson?" Carley gaped. "Someone set the fire? They wanted to kill me, didn't they?"

Russ hesitated and then nodded, his expression compassionate. "It looks that way. But we're going to do all we can to keep that from happening."

Carley sighed. "You can't always be here. It's just luck the alarm woke me this time."

Russ nodded. He glanced at Blake. "You taking her with you?"

Martha answered for him. "Yes, we are. And we need to be going."

"Good idea. She'll be safe there. I'll talk to you later, Carley." Russ watched them walk to the car.

When they reached the house, his mother led Carley inside and whisked her upstairs. Blake sat down in the living room and contemplated all that had happened. From what he could see, Carley's house had suffered a lot of damage. He hoped she had enough insurance to cover the loss. She had enough to deal with, and then this.

He heard his mom and Carley coming and tried to wipe the concern off his face. She needed to relax, get some rest. Later today would be soon enough to face all she'd lost and try to make sense of it.

Carley wore a pair of jeans he recognized as his mother's, about two inches too short, but the elastic waistband fit. She'd need to go shopping for clothes, shoes ... everything. She picked up her purse she'd placed on the footstool and sat down on the divan behind the coffee table. "This is all I have left, I guess. Everything else is either gone or ruined."

His mother sat down beside Carley and patted her hand. "It will work out, dear. Just put it in God's hands and trust him to lead you. And you're not alone. You have us. We'll help you all we can."

Blake nodded. Yes, she had them, and from what he'd seen, she had a lot of people from church who would jump in to help too. Westfield Community Faith Church had a lot of good people who were quick to lend a hand where needed.

Carley opened her purse and reached inside. "I need to call Juanita and tell her I won't be at work today. It's early, I know, but she won't mind."

She fumbled around without finding the phone. "Well, where is it? It's not in the pocket where I usually keep it." Finally, looking frustrated, she grabbed the bag by the bottom and upended it on the coffee table in front of her. The contents clattered out in a pile. She had to stop stuffing things in without taking time to put them in the proper place. She'd bought this thing because it had so many compartments, and now, she couldn't find anything when she needed it.

Blake's attention was drawn to the mess she'd just made. How on earth had she managed to get all of that in her purse? No wonder it was so heavy.

His eyes focused on what he was seeing. Two phones? "Do you have two phones?"

Carley shook her head. "No, I only have one."

Hands trembling, she reached for the iPhone with the teal case and pushed it aside. "That one's mine."

She pushed the home button on the second phone. A picture of her and Nancy from a few years back held her attention for a few moments, but then she looked at Blake. "This is Nancy's phone. She must have dropped it in my purse by mistake that night in the park."

Blake nodded, his lips clamped shut. Could this be what the guy out to get Carley was looking for? "I guess that's why Russ couldn't find it."

"Probably so. Nancy said she'd taken a picture of the man with Rachel Blevins. It has to be on here."

Carley thumbed through the stored pictures, stopping and staring as if in disbelief at what she saw. She looked at them, her voice shaking. "Kurt. It's Kurt Lister, and he's with Rachel Blevins. He's the killer. He has to be. And this is what he's been trying to find. He must have Nancy's purse and known the phone was missing."

Blake leaned over and took the phone from her. There it was. The answer to the puzzle. Kurt held the woman by the shoulder, and she was staring at the camera, her eyes large with fear. Kurt was staring too—glaring, really. In fact, his expression justified what Nancy had told Carley about the way he had looked at her. Blake reached for his cell phone, punching in Russ' number.

They waited in silence for the few minutes it took for Russ to arrive. There didn't seem to be anything to say. The investigation was winding down, and not in the way any of them had expected. A car pulled into the driveway, and Blake went to the door. Russ strode up the walk, his eyes lined with dark circles and his mouth downturned in exhaustion. He didn't bother greeting him, just stepped past Blake as he moved back out of the way.

"Okay, what's this all about?"

Carley nodded toward Blake. "He has the phone. He'll show you."

Russ turned his attention to Blake, who handed the phone to him. He sank into a chair, staring at the picture. "Kurt Lister? The killer is Kurt Lister? Why would he do something like that?"

"Well, think about this." Blake held up his hand as Russ started to speak. "Just remember who he's married to. Marlene Lister owns Barnes Manufacturing, and you can bet she controls most of the money. If you were as arrogant and self-important as Kurt is, would you want some young woman you'd been seeing pushing for marriage? He had too much to lose. No way would he have wanted Marlene to find out."

"But that's not the first time Kurt's cheated, if the local gossip is true." Russ objected. "She had to have heard some of it."

"She probably did, but it was just gossip. She could ignore it. She couldn't ignore a younger woman trying to take her husband."

"That's true, but somehow I'd expect her to take care of the problem, not Kurt."

Blake glanced down at the phone. "I've got a hunch he was desperate. If his affair got out, Marlene would have dumped him and not looked back. Her pride wouldn't let her put up with anything like that. And when he killed Rachel, he put himself in jeopardy. If he got caught, he'd be headed for prison, maybe the death penalty."

Russ shook his head. "The guy had it made, but he just couldn't leave well enough alone. I'll put an APB on him. We'll try to bring him in before he pulls anything else."

Russ stepped out into the foyer to make a phone call, then entered the room again. "Look, I've got to be going. Stay in touch and if you need help, call. I'll have someone here as soon as possible."

Russ left and Carley looked at Blake. "If we need help? What does he think will happen?"

"I don't know, but I'm going to make sure the doors are locked before we go to bed."

Martha had been quiet but she interrupted as Blake walked toward the front door. "Have you looked at the clock? It's already five a.m. I know we've had a rough night, but it's too late for me to go back to bed. It'll soon be time for breakfast, but the two of you feel free to catch up on your sleep if you like. I can stand guard."

Blake glanced at his watch. Yep. Five o'clock. If he crawled back into bed, as tired as he was, he'd probably sleep all day. A picture flashed through his mind. At the fire, he'd seen someone who looked familiar ... a man. But before he'd got a good look, the guy had turned and walked away. He'd worn a cap, the brim pulled down low, and his face hadn't been clear, but the more Blake thought about it, the man could have been Kurt Lister. Blake's blood ran hot, then cold. Kurt had come *that* close to killing her last night. No matter what it took, Blake was going to find that cold-hearted killer and when he did, he'd make him pay for this night's work.

After breakfast he took Carley back to the charred remains of her house. The roof was mostly gone, including the back part of the house—where her bedroom had been located—which, after last night, stood without any covering. The front part of the house was smoked, the walls standing but without any support. She wasn't going to be able to salvage much.

Carley stood staring at what was left of her home, her shoulders bowed and tears blurring her eyes. He put his arm around her, drawing her close. "You're not alone. Mom and I will help, and so will the people at church. We'll see you through this. I promise it'll be all right. Somehow, we'll make it work."

She turned, burying her face against him. He could feel the wetness of her tears. For several minutes they stood like that until she pulled away. "Thank you. I feel so lost, so confused. I don't know what to do first."

"Don't try to do anything today. You're not in any condition to make plans just yet. Give yourself a little time and stay with us until we get things straightened out. You'll want to go shopping, get some clothes, whatever you need for the time being. How does that sound?"

She gave him the first real smile she'd managed. It quivered a little around the edges, but it was a smile. He knew in his heart that this woman would be strong enough to make it through the blow life had handed her, and he'd be there to help her.

God would be there too.

He turned her toward the car. "There's nothing we can do here. Let's go back to the house, and you and Mom can go shopping. I've got a few things to do."

Like finding Kurt Lister. The guy had to be stopped before he did anything else.

Chapter Sixteen

Carley and Martha hit the thrift shops, coming away with several pairs of jeans and dressier pants, tops, sweatshirts, and a couple of jackets. Undergarments and sleepwear, they bought at the local Walmart. They had reached home and Carley had loaded the washer with some of her clothes when the doorbell rang. Martha opened the door to find Marlene Lister.

Carley hurried to the living room, expecting the other woman to be in a rage over the accusation that her husband was a killer, but Marlene looked subdued, even a little nervous.

She glanced at Carley. "May I talk to you for a minute?"

"Of course. Let's sit down."

The three women sank into chairs, and Martha and Carley waited for their guest to pull herself together. Marlene sat for a few moments, eyes downcast and her lower lip tucked in, before sighing and looking at them in turn. "I suppose you're wondering why I'm here."

Martha nodded. "The thought had crossed my mind."

"I had a visit from Russ Pryor last night. He wanted to know where Kurt was. I had to tell him I had no idea."

"What do you mean, you have no idea? He's your husband. Wasn't he home with you?"

Marlene shook her head. "No. He left around eleven thirty. I heard him go. He never came back."

"You haven't heard from him?" Martha had evidently taken charge, and Carley was content to sit back and let her ask the questions.

"I haven't talked to him since around nine last night. He went to bed early, said he was tired, but then he left later, so he must not have been that tired to start with."

"I see."

Marlene's cheeks reddened. "No, you don't see. What you don't understand is that in the beginning, I really loved him. Kurt ... well, he can be very charming when he wants to be."

Carley remembered how he had fooled her. She had even started to like him despite Blake's words and was a little angry at Marlene over the way she treated him. She was beginning to realize that maybe Marlene had a reason for her behavior.

"Then he began to change, always wanting more control. That's why I never put his name on the business. Actually, I finally came to realize all Kurt really cared about was himself. It was a constant battle. Then he started cheating."

She blinked back tears. "I wanted our marriage to work, but I finally realized it never would, so I decided to reclaim my life, to ignore him the way he ignored me."

Carley leaned forward. "But you seemed so much in control, so sure of yourself. I never suspected…" In fact, she had felt sorry for Kurt.

Marlene took a deep breath and sighed again. "We're each two different persons—the way we are in public and the way we are in private. Not all marriages are made in heaven."

"I suppose not."

Martha had stopped talking, just sitting there, alert, taking in every word. Marlene swallowed, blinking back tears. "After the wedding I was going to make him an equal partner in the business, but we hadn't been married much over a week when I caught him going behind my back, countermanding my orders, telling my employees he was in charge. After that, I was afraid to give him any authority."

Carley listened to this woman she had thought was hard, arrogant, and overbearing, and understood her a little better. Like other people she knew, Marlene had been struggling, fighting to hold on to what should have been hers—a husband she had already lost. She understood Kurt a little better too. He was the one who had been hard and arrogant, believing he could do what he pleased with no consequences. Anyone who got in his way was ruthlessly dealt with, even if it meant murder.

She shivered at the thought.

"What will you do if you hear from him?" Martha asked.

"I'll try to find out where he is and call Russ, of course. I'm through with Kurt. From what I hear, that girl … Rachel … was young, inexperienced, probably trusted him to do what he promised. He took advantage of her. He's on his own now. I don't want anything to do with him, and if there is any way I can help catch him, I'll do it."

Carley, listening closely, was sure she detected a ring of truth in Marlene's voice. Who could blame her, married to a power-hungry, cheating killer? Another thought occurred to Carley and she immediately put it into words.

"Are you sure you're safe? After all, that piece of machinery almost hit both of us."

"I've thought of that. I suspect he had some way of knowing where we were standing when he caused that thing to fall. I've had men at the plant checking that deck, trying to find out what happened. They've discovered the deck was on some kind of heavy hinges activated by a control inside the office. So, yes, since I stood in the way of him being able to do exactly what he wanted, I have a feeling I was supposed to die too.

"My father built that plant and that deck was already there when I took over. I had enough to deal with. Checking every detail of a building that had always worked wasn't on my list."

"Do you think you're safe now?" Carley pressed. Since Kurt had shown a strong streak of self-preservation and a determination to punish anyone who crossed him, what would keep him from coming after the wife who had denied him the power he desired?

"No, I don't, which is why I have men at the house and traveling with me. A couple of them are waiting for me out in the car. If he knows what's good for him, he'll stay away from me."

A touch of her former arrogance had returned, and Carley had a feeling Marlene would do just fine. She wouldn't let a little thing like a cheating husband slow her down. Carley felt a grudging respect for the woman. She hoped she could be as strong as Marlene Lister. However, she didn't have guards to protect her. She didn't even have a home anymore.

Marlene got to her feet. "I appreciate you seeing me. I just want to make it clear that I'll do absolutely nothing to protect Kurt. But you need to be careful. He might still be in the area. If he is, you're not safe."

"We're assuming he is," Martha said. "Although I was surprised that he was our killer. I would never have guessed it."

Marlene shook her head and sighed. "Neither would I—and I'm married to him."

"One more thing." Carley ran her fingers through her hair. "I've felt uncomfortable at work. As if something was going on behind my back. But I can't see any connection between Kurt and Mr. Quigley."

Marlene laughed. "You can't? Well believe me, it's there. Sherman Quigley is Kurt's father. Illegitimate, of course. He didn't even really get acquainted with him until Kurt was twelve. Since then, Sherman has done all he could to help him make it. He's the one who introduced us, although I didn't know until several years later that they were related."

Carley stared at her, stunned. "His father?"

"That's right, and Daddy will do anything necessary to protect his little boy. If I were you, I'd stay away from Quigley Enterprises."

Marlene left, and Carley slumped in her chair, staring helplessly at Martha. "Is anyone what they seem to be? Marlene, Kurt, Mr. Quigley…"

Martha shook her head. "I think most of us are what the occasion calls for. We can never know anyone completely, even the people we care about. Even ourselves."

"Are you saying we can't trust anyone?"

"No, I'm just saying we don't always know people as well as we think we do. But right now, our main focus needs to be on staying alive. You don't go out of this house unless I know where you're going and with whom. We have to be careful. Marlene was right on that."

Blake came home for lunch, and they filled him in on their conversation with Marlene. "So she thinks he meant to kill both of you. All the more reason to get him before he can do anything else."

After they ate, he asked Carley if she wanted to go for a drive.

Carley jumped at the idea. She loved Martha and was grateful for the way she was being sheltered and taken care of, but she wanted to go by and look at her house again. Just get out for a while.

She offered to do the dishes first, but Martha shook her head. "You go ahead. It will do you good, and as for the dishes, there're not all that many. I don't need any help with them."

Carley smiled and looked at Blake. "I guess I'm ready to go."

They walked out to the car and got in. Carley fastened her seatbelt. "Where are we going?"

Blake shrugged. "Wherever you want to go. I thought we'd drive by what's left of your house if you wanted to and then maybe go down by the lake and just take it easy for an hour or so. Give you a chance to get away from it all."

"That sounds good." Carley relaxed against the seat, happy to be spending time with Blake. They never seemed to be alone together anymore.

They got out and walked around the house. The damage was worse at the back, right where she had been sleeping. Carley shivered at how close she'd come to becoming the third victim of Kurt Lister's attacks. She had a hunch God played a big part in her safety from the fire. He'd been taking care of her so far. She prayed he would continue to shelter her.

After inspecting what was left of her house, they drove around for a while, just talking. Mostly they avoided mentioning the thing uppermost on their minds—Kurt and what he was doing. Blake turned into the road leading to a small lake at the edge of town.

At the lake, they got out of the car and strolled down to the water. A duck was swimming a short distance from shore, leaving a rippled wake behind, its brown breast and green head shining in the golden rays of the sun. A blue heron stalked the opposite shore and the song of a mocking bird serenaded them. Carley breathed deeply of the fresh air. The beauty of the scene and the peacefulness of God's creation were a balm to her soul. Here she could relax, put aside the things that were troubling her. Reclaim herself.

Blake held her hand and she rejoiced in the warmth of his touch, the comfort of his presence. She longed to tell him how she felt, but she was afraid to. What if he didn't feel the same about her? Yes, he held her hand, was there when she needed him, but she wasn't sure if that was the way he felt about her, or if it was just the sort of person he was. Sometimes she believed he cared, but then she would realize she wasn't good enough for him. She never would be.

They sat down on a rock, the sun warm on their backs and a gentle breeze caressing their faces. Carley stared across the water, seeing the small dark head of something swimming. Beaver? Muskrat? She couldn't tell. She sat quietly, soaking up the silence, the peacefulness.

Blake cleared his throat. "There's something I want to talk to you about."

She turned her head to look at him. "What?"

He hesitated and she had a feeling he was uncomfortable about whatever was on his mind. What was he going to bring up?

He glanced away, looking out at the water and then back at her. "Tell me what happened when your parents died."

She stared at him in disbelief. "What? Why would you bring that up?"

Blake looked directly into her eyes. "You've changed. More serious, more thoughtful, not the way I remember you. What caused it?"

"You think my parents' death did?"

He nodded. "I'm beginning to think so. Do you want to talk about it?"

Did she? No, she didn't. That was the one thing she never talked about. Couldn't bear to, but something in his expression … compassion … or something deeper, made her think it would be all right to tell him.

"Hasn't anyone told you about it?"

"No. I asked Mom and she said I needed to ask you. I haven't asked anyone else."

"You've heard something about it though, haven't you?"

"At the fire. A couple of women. One was sorry for you. The other said you had killed your parents."

Carley flinched as if he had struck her. She knew some people still felt that way, and it was true, she couldn't deny that. She tightened her lips and looked away from him.

"It's hard to talk about."

"Then you don't have to. It's all right, Carley."

"No, it isn't. You've done so much for me, and you have a right to know the truth. I'm not what you think. You need to know the real me."

"I know you and I like you just the way you are."

"Wait until I finish before you judge. You remember what I was like in high school. Running wild, me and Nancy both, always on the edge of trouble. We were into drugs and alcohol."

"That's in the past, Carley. You've changed."

She laughed bitterly. "The past is always with us. It's a part of us."

He waited, not sure if he wanted to hear it.

She gripped her hands tightly together and licked her lips. "Nancy's brother was in deeper than we were. He died of an overdose and Nancy stopped using. Stopped cold. But I didn't … didn't want to." She stopped fighting tears. "My parents … they tried to talk to me, but I wouldn't listen. Oh, I knew they disapproved and were disappointed in me, and I guess they kept hoping I would see how foolish I was being and straighten up."

Blake didn't say anything, and somehow, that gave her the strength to go on. "There was a meeting about addiction at a church—not ours, but another one, out of town. They ordered me to go with them. That made me angry. I downed a couple of pills just to show them something. I have no idea what. Just showing off, I guess, but they didn't even know about it. I insisted they let me drive or else I wouldn't go. I suppose driving gave me some sense of control."

Blake reached over and took her hand. She blinked and continued. "My father was telling me I had to behave at the meeting, keep quiet, no mouthing off. I was angry, yelling back at him. It was a foggy night. I wasn't paying attention the way I should have been. I started to turn onto a side road, refusing to go any farther, just acting on an impulse, not thinking of what I was doing.

"A truck popped over the hill just as I started to make a turn. My father yelled for me to look out. I meant to slam on the brake. Instead I stomped on the gas. The truck hit us. They both died instantly. I spent a couple of weeks in the hospital, wishing I had died with them."

"But it was an accident."

"It was my fault. I know that. I've had a hard time living with it, and some people have made it clear they hold it against me. I really can't blame them for it either." Her voice choked and she swallowed hard, not sure she could go on. "I can still hear my mother screaming."

"How did you end up in church?"

Carley managed a smile, although it didn't feel natural. "Your mother. She wouldn't leave me alone. She had people praying for me, called me every

Saturday, trying to talk me into going with her. I finally gave in, just to get her off my back. I've been going ever since."

Blake reached for her, pulling her against him. "Look, Carley, what happened was bad, but it's over. You can't keep shouldering this burden. Have you asked God to forgive you? He will, you know. All you have to do is ask."

"Of course I've asked Him. Over and over. But somehow, I don't feel forgiven. I've messed up too many lives. Nancy didn't start doing drugs until I pushed her into trying them. I destroy everyone I care about."

Blake got to his feet, pulling her up with him, sorry he had pushed her into talking. He should have asked Russ or someone else about her parents' deaths, but he had honestly felt she needed to talk about the accident.

He rested his cheek in her hair, as soft and silky as a rose petal, searching for something to say. "Don't, Carley. Nancy's death wasn't your fault. You didn't know someone was after her, and you didn't know he would kill her. She put you in danger, not the other way around."

She drew back and stared up at him. "But I should have done something."

"What could you do? He had a gun. You didn't. There was nothing you could have done."

Blake could see her thinking about this, but he knew she wasn't convinced. He hoped with time she could see it. For the time being, he had to help her as much as he could. Help her find peace within her heart and mind, and keep her safe. He'd gotten his orders that morning, although he hadn't said anything about it. He had to report for duty in a couple of weeks. He had to know she was safe before he left. Had to know Kurt Lister was behind bars where he belonged.

Right then, though, he had to comfort her the best he could. "Look, Carley. If you've asked God to forgive you, then He has. He promised he would forgive us if we just ask, and He doesn't lie. What you need to do now is forgive yourself."

She gazed up at him, and something twisted inside him as he saw the hurt and vulnerability in her expression. "How do I do that? Tell me."

He drew a deep breath, thinking. "You ask Him to help you. He'll never let you down, Carley. I believe He has forgiven you—it's your turn now. Realize that what happened was a long time ago. It's over. It's time to move past it and reclaim your life. Time to wake up to the blessings God has in store for you."

She looked up at him, her eyes blurred with tears. "I can't ... I can't."

"You can, Carley. Pray about it and I'll pray for you too. Ask and you shall receive. It's God's promise." He had some inkling of how she felt about her parents and Nancy. He might not have been able to forgive himself either.

His phone sounded and he tried to ignore it, but she wouldn't let him. "You'd better answer that."

He nodded and dug it out of his pocket. The voice sounding in his ear was familiar. Kurt Lister. "Hey, Blake. You having fun with Carley? I can see you real clear. Sure wish I had a gun. I'll have one next time. You tell that little tramp I'm going to fix her for showing the police that phone. She'll regret that. So will you."

Blake ended the call and grabbed Carley. "Let's get out of here."

"Why? Who was that?"

"Kurt. He's here. Said he could see us. Head for the car." He got her in front of him, hoping he was shielding her. Kurt might have said he didn't have a gun, but that didn't mean he was telling the truth. After all, he wasn't known for being all that honest. Blake had to get Carley out of there. If he had been by himself he would have tried to find that jerk, but not when Carley was with him.

They reached the car and got inside. No bullets had exploded, so maybe Kurt was telling the truth this time. He turned the car and headed back the way they had come. From that point on, they were being more careful of where they went. He should have known better than to come out to a secluded place like this. But how had Kurt known where they were? No one else did.

Carley was quiet. He didn't know if she was thinking of what he had said about forgiveness or if she was worried at the idea of Kurt being so close. He should have minded his own business, but just the same, he believed he was right. She needed to forgive herself. He headed the car toward home, but as soon as he got Carley safe, he was going to sit down and think about where Kurt could be hiding out, and he was going to find him if it was the last thing he ever did.

Chapter Seventeen

Blake took Carley to his house, and she wandered out into the backyard to sit in the sunshine. She was still disturbed by what had happened in the park. Where had Kurt been hiding? She wouldn't be sitting there, alive and scared. And yes, she was scared; only a fool wouldn't be.

Her phone rang and she answered automatically. The voice she heard chilled her blood.

"Hey, Carley. You thinking about me? You'd better be. I'm your worst nightmare."

"Why are you doing this, Kurt? I never did anything to you."

"You gave Russ that phone."

"You started threatening me long before that. Why?"

"Why? You dare ask me that? You were a threat to everything I had. I knew you had to have that phone. It was just a matter of time before you found it. You've destroyed me. I'm a marked man because of you. I've lost my wife, my business, everything, and it's all your fault. You could have saved me. Instead, you chose to destroy me. And now, I'm going to take care of you. You'll never be safe as long as I'm alive."

Carley refused to let him know the terror he inspired. "I'm not afraid of you, Kurt."

"Well, now, that's a mistake. Look at what happened to Nancy. You don't want to end up like her, do you—dead on the side of the road?"

"You killed two women. If you cared so much for your wife, why did you cheat on her?"

"It wasn't her I cared about. It was the money. I'd be gone from the Barnes family and all it meant and all the cash. Marlene would have kicked me out without a dime. I'd have lost everything that mattered. Then that meddling woman—Nancy—took my picture with Rachel, and I knew it was all over. She'd never have kept it to herself. Not after Rachel was found dead."

"You tried to kill me and Marlene both that day at the plant, didn't you?"

"And I'd have succeeded if you hadn't walked away when you did. If that motor had hit both of you, I'd have been safe. No one would have connected me to Nancy, and I'd be in charge of the plant. Just the way I should be. But you had to get in my way. I can't let you get away with that."

The hatred in his voice sent a shiver through Carley. She'd never experienced anything this evil before. *Help me out here, God.* She didn't know how to handle a situation like that. A hand reached over her shoulder, taking the phone. She twisted around to see Blake standing there looking furious.

He listened, then opened his mouth and started talking. "Look, Kurt. You've killed two women and tried to kill two more. There's no way you can get by with doing something like that. You may as well turn yourself in because you're going to get caught. And I'm going to do my best to help that happen."

Kurt's voice was so loud and so full of venom Carley could hear it even though she no longer held the phone. "You stay out of this, Richards. It's none of your business."

"I'm making it my business. Stay away from Carley if you know what's good for you."

He ended the call before Kurt could say anything more. "Russ needs to know about this and about that call in the park. There has to be some way he knows where we are most of the time."

Carley glanced around the yard, halfway expecting to see Kurt, although she knew he wasn't there. It wasn't a large yard, and a board fence with pointed ends stood about six feet high. No way could he see her. On second thought, he hadn't mentioned being able to see, and he hadn't talked like he knew she was in Blake's backyard. So could he only see them sometimes, only know where they were occasionally, not all the time?

Her phone rang again and Blake handed it to her. Mr. Quigley. "Miss Sutherland? Do you think you can just drift in and out of here whenever you want to show up?"

"No, I..."

He interrupted her. "I gave you every chance to advance with this company and you have continually shown a lack of regard for me and your position here. I will not put up with this sort of behavior. You're fired."

"Fired?"

"You heard me. And you have forfeited your final paycheck. I never want to see you in this plant again."

He ended the call and Carley looked up at Blake, her eyes wide. "He fired me."

"Well, that's not a bad thing. He might be mixed up in this some way. After all, he's the one who sent you out to the plant where you almost got killed."

Carley huffed out a sigh. "I was so upset after finding Nancy's phone that I guess I just forgot to call Juanita. I was planning to quit anyway, but I don't like being fired. I didn't deserve that."

"He's probably angry because you found Nancy's phone and set the cops on his son. At least, Marlene claims he's Quigley's son. I guess she would know the truth about that. She's married to Kurt."

"I'm sure she does. She seemed different, more vulnerable. I actually felt sorry for her."

"That would be something new. I don't know that I've ever felt sorry for Marlene. She always seemed to have it all together."

Carley shook her head. "She said something that made me think. I mentioned that she always seemed to be in control, and she said we are all different people in public than we are in private. Two different personalities. I think she's right. None of us behaves in public the way we sometimes behave in private."

"I guess that's true. It fits Kurt, anyway. I'm going to call Russ and tell him about these phone calls you're getting—he needs to know."

"All right. I'm going to sit out here and soak up some sun. I'll be in later."

Blake left and Carley leaned back in her chair, staring up at the sky. She had a lot to think about—about Kurt and his plan to kill her, about getting fired from her job. She also needed to think about what Blake had said about forgiving herself. Good advice, but she didn't know how to go about accomplishing it. She was going to need some help from God with that.

A while later Kara opened the gate and entered the yard, looking like she would break down and cry any minute. Carley got to her feet and reached to hug her. "What's wrong?"

Kara batted her eyes against the tears and took a deep breath. Carley led her to a chair. "Let's sit down and you can tell me all about it."

Kara sat down and leaned back. She glanced away, obviously struggling to get herself under control. After a minute, she looked back at Carley. "I didn't know where you were staying, so I called that policeman, Russ, and he told me you were here. I could have called on your cell, but I needed to see you and make sure you were all right. I'm so sorry about your house, but I'm thankful you weren't hurt." She blinked again as tears started to fall. "It's Nate. He got a job offer in Texas. He wanted me to go with him—not to get married, but to live together. I told him I couldn't do that."

"No, of course not. That's not something you would do."

"I tried to talk to him, but he got angry. Told me to choose between him and God." She wiped her eyes.

Carley moved to kneel in front of her. "Oh, Kara. I'm so sorry. Is he still here?"

"No, he left this morning. He was angry, wouldn't listen to reason. It had to be his way or no way. He wouldn't listen to my side at all. From what he said, he blames God. Nate thinks I've been brainwashed into believing in something that doesn't exist."

She licked her lips and swallowed. "I don't get it. If God doesn't exist, then how could it be God's fault we're not getting along? That doesn't make sense."

Carley grasped Kara's hand. "People who don't believe in God don't make much sense. But I understand. He asked you to turn your back on everything you believe, but he couldn't even offer you marriage in return. Of course you couldn't accept an offer like that."

"But I feel so awful. I love him, but he loves his lifestyle more than he cares about me. That hurts."

"I know it does, and I'll be praying for you, but you made the right decision. I believe God has something good in store for you, Kara. Just put your trust in Him and keep living what you believe. Nate may not have been the right man for you."

That was what she had thought all along. He was too rough, too sure of himself. Kara deserved someone better, someone who shared her love for God. A Bible verse flickered through her mind, something about not being unequally yoked with unbelievers. Kara needed to wait. The right man would come along eventually. Better to be alone than tied to the wrong one.

Kara wiped her eyes. "I don't see how he could leave knowing the man who is trying to kill both of us is still out there. I wish the police would catch him and end this terrible mess we're in."

"I do too. As you know, I've lost my home, but if you are afraid, I'm sure Martha and Blake would insist you stay here."

Kara looked tempted, but then she shook her head. "I'll not lie, it would feel safer, but I'd rather be in my own house. I don't want this creep pushing me out of my own home."

Carley knew how Kara felt. She'd been the same way, refusing to let this jerk drive her from her home. And look what had happened. He'd destroyed her home. She had no place of her own, no personal belongings, nothing that had belonged to her parents. He'd taken it all from her. He could do the same to Kara. She started to say so but stopped when Kara held up her hand.

"I know what you're going to say, Carley, but it's no use. I may be putting myself in danger by staying in my home, but that's the way it is right now. I'm not going to let him drive me out. I may regret it later, but I'll deal with it. I had an alarm installed, and Rex, my German Shepherd, will protect me. Plus, I have a gun. That's the best I can do right now."

Carley clamped her lips together in a rueful smile and nodded. "I do understand. I just want you to be safe."

"You can't guarantee my safety. No one can. I appreciate the way you feel, but I can't live in a box. I have to be out in the world. I'll stay in touch, and I promise to tell you if anything goes wrong."

After she left, Carley went into the house, not wanting to be alone outside any longer. She helped Martha with a few things, insisted on washing the dishes after dinner, and then Blake cornered her in the living room. Martha joined them, sitting in her usual chair with her hands resting casually on the arms, but Carley noticed her alert expression and the direct focus of her eyes.

Blake closed the living room curtains and took a seat on the couch. "Okay, now let's talk. What did Kara want?"

"Nate has left town. He got a job and wanted Kara to go with him, but since he didn't offer marriage, she refused."

Martha nodded in approval. "Wise decision."

Blake ignored this. "She's in danger. Why would he leave now?"

Carley shrugged. "I guess he cared more for the job than he did for Kara."

He glanced questioningly at his mother and she nodded. He switched his attention to Carley. "She can move in here with us. She'd have to share a room with you, but you wouldn't mind, would you?"

"No, I wouldn't mind, but I mentioned the possibility to her and she refused to consider it. She said no one was going to drive her out of her home."

Blake heaved a sigh. "That's a foolish attitude. She's just asking for trouble."

"The way I did?"

"I didn't say that."

"But you were thinking it. And considering what happened, I guess you were right. I'd hate for anything to happen to Kara, but I do understand how she feels."

"That won't help much if her house burns too."

"I know. I'm worried about that. You can call her if you want and see if you can talk some sense into her. I've done all I can."

They went to their rooms shortly after that, but Carley couldn't sleep. Finally, she did what she usually did during restless nights—got out of bed to stand at the window, staring out at the moon-silvered yard. Blake's words came back to her. She needed to forgive herself, but she didn't know how to go about it.

Carley stared up at the sky, the round globe of the silver moon, the stars. *God, are you there?* She breathed hard, as if she had been running. *I just don't know what to do right now. I want to get rid of this burden of guilt I've carried for so long, but I'm confused about what to do about it. Help me out here.*

She didn't receive an answer, but she didn't really expect one. It was something she had to do on her own. She thought back over the years to the night of the accident. Yes, it had been her fault. She couldn't deny that. But it hadn't been intentional. She had loved her parents, even though she had put them through a lot of hurt and disappointment.

Tears rolled down her face, and she swiped them away with her hand. She'd come this far, and she wouldn't quit until she worked her way through. She thought of the people at church, how some had condemned her and others had prayed for her. Of the many times she had cried out to God, asking Him to forgive her. According to Blake, He already had. She was asking to be forgiven for something God had already taken care of. It was time to stop, time to let it go. If only she could.

Carley bowed her head, leaving herself open to any leading from God. *Please, show me the way. Help me forgive myself. Take this away from me and let me live trusting in your love and forgiveness.*

Gradually a sense of peacefulness crept through her. A load had been lifted. Tears filled her eyes again. She felt … whole, replenished. God had healed her. She bowed her head again, thanking Him for what He had done for her.

After a few more minutes just standing in front of the window, soaking in the peace and joy, she made her way back to the bed. She could sleep. Tomorrow was another day, and with God's help she would face whatever came.

Blake talked to Russ about the phone calls and then got on the computer. He was going to find out everything he could about Kurt Lister, including any friends he might have. But then, after considering it, he couldn't remember ever seeing Kurt with a group of men, or even an occasional male friend. On thinking it over, he realized he really didn't know much about Kurt. Well, he would know more before the day was over.

An hour later he looked at the stack of papers he'd printed out. He'd learned a lot, but nothing that would tell where Kurt could be hiding out. According to Russ, the police hadn't run across anything that would help them either. Russ had helped him check both his and Carley's cars, and had found the tracking devices that had helped Kurt know where they were. They'd removed the one from Carley's and then they checked Kara's car and removed hers too, but for the time being, he'd left the device on his car. Maybe it would lure Kurt out of hiding. At least, he hoped it would. They needed to catch him before he struck again.

The following morning Blake smiled at Carley from across the breakfast table. "I've got to make a run down to Harrisburg today. Want to come along for the ride?"

Harrisburg was a bustling town an hour's drive away through hills, valleys, and trees, with a splendid view everywhere you looked.

"Of course I want to go. It will be wonderful to get away from here for a few hours. I'd love it." She looked at Blake's mother, whose eyebrows were raised in question.

Martha shook her head. "Don't look at me. That curvy road gives me a bad case of motion sickness. You couldn't drag me into the car. The two of you go along and have fun. I'll hold down the home front."

Carley shot her a concerned glance. "Will you be all right?"

"Of course. Why wouldn't I be? Oh, I see. You think Kurt may show up and take his anger out on me. Well, let him come. I can handle Kurt Lister."

Blake frowned at her. "Now don't do anything foolish. You can't handle someone like Kurt. You catch even a glimpse of him, you call Russ. That's an order."

Martha made a face at him. "That's the way it is. You raise them and the first thing you know, they're giving orders and expecting you to obey them."

Blake laughed. "I realize you're not very good at taking orders, but you obey that one. This guy isn't anything to mess with. Now, will you call Russ if you see anything out of order?"

Martha frowned. "All right, I promise. I'll be careful."

"All right. Now, you stick with that and you'll be okay." He looked at Carley. "How soon can you be ready to go?"

"Right now, I guess."

He looked at her, smiling. She had put on one of her nicer pairs of jeans and a light blue sweater. Her hair hung loose on her shoulders. He knew she wasn't dressing up for his benefit. She just wanted to look nice in her former teacher's home. Nevertheless, her pretty features endeared her to him even more.

In a few minutes they were in Blake's car, heading out of town. The sun shone golden rays that brought the world to life. Birds fluttered in the trees they passed, and lacy clouds floated in a bright blue sky. Blake grinned. A special day to spend with Carley. It didn't get any better than this. The road dropped into a valley and around a curve, then began to climb a steep slope.

As the car crested the hill, he noticed Carley looking out her window at the sheer drop on her side of the road. Trees dotted the hillside, and he glimpsed green fields in the distance. Suddenly he noticed a black SUV behind them, coming fast.

Carley jerked around to stare at him. "Blake, someone's behind us. It could be Kurt." Her eyes were wide with fear.

He glanced in the rearview mirror again. The guy was coming right at them and getting closer. "Quick, call Russ. Tell him where we are and what's going on."

If this was Kurt, help would be too far away to do them much good. They were on their own, but at least Russ would know Kurt was after them.

Carley gave Russ their location. Before she finished the call, the SUV pulled alongside them and slammed into the side of their car.

Carley screamed and Blake fought the wheel, trying to stay on the road. The car slipped off the road and careened downhill, its front end slamming into a tree.

Blake managed to get out of the car, then reached in to pull Carley out. He hauled her through the open door and practically dragged her toward a stand of trees. A rock shelf jutted out of the hillside, and Blake nodded in that direction. Slowly, carefully, they crawled under the shelter of the rock. A car door slammed above them. In the distance came the faint wail of sirens. Russ? No, it couldn't be. He hadn't had time to get here. But at least someone was on the way. He hoped they arrived before Kurt reached them. If not, Kurt would kill them.

Carley could hear someone coming down the hill, sliding and scrambling to keep his footing. The sirens came closer. Blake threw himself over her, shielding her with his body. Carley tried to push him off. She would not allow him to sacrifice himself for her. She loved him too much.

The footsteps moved closer. She could turn her head and see a small part of the area behind them. Kurt stood there with a gun in his hand.

"Stand up!"

His voice grated in her ears. She felt Blake rise slowly to his knees. He got to his feet and despite the pain, she managed to struggle upright. Cars stopped overhead. Doors slammed. Voices shouted.

Distracted, Kurt shot a glance upward and Blake limped toward him, going much too slowly. Kurt jerked his head around to face him. "Stop right there."

Blake ignored the command, moving faster. Kurt raised the gun and Carley lunged forward, trying to reach them. "Blake … no!"

Kurt pulled the trigger.

Blake fell.

Carley screamed and ran toward him. She stumbled, staggered, then caught her balance. She had to reach Blake. Kurt yelled something, but she didn't catch it. Didn't pay attention. A gun blasted close at hand. Then another. She heard someone fall, but she was too focused on Blake to pay attention.

He lay still, blood running from a wound at the side of his head. She knelt beside him, calling his name. Hands grasped her, lifting her out of the way. She struggled against them, trying to fight before realizing the man holding her was a policeman.

He nodded at her. "You're safe now. Just relax. We'll take care of him."

Carley made an effort to calm down, and he released her. She turned and saw Kurt lying several feet away, not moving. Two policemen were standing over him. An ambulance arrived and the men placed Blake on a stretcher. Carley followed them as they carried him up the hillside, praying all the way. Soon she was inside an ambulance speeding down the hill, siren screaming. The guy in the ambulance checked a gash on her forehead, but other than that, her injuries were minor compared to Blake's and Kurt's. Russ was waiting at the hospital when she arrived and sat with her while she stared out the window and prayed.

An hour passed with no information before the doctor appeared and told them Blake would be fine. The bullet had only grazed his skull, but they were going to keep him overnight. A nurse led Carley to his room where he lay on the bed, pale but awake. He smiled when he saw her, and she pulled up a chair and sat down. His hand was warm in hers, and she sighed a silent prayer of thanksgiving that he was safe.

His expression changed, becoming serious. "I'm sorry, Carley. I knew about the tracking thing he'd put on my car. I messed up."

She gripped his hand, trying to find the courage to say the words clogging her throat. Finally, she licked her lips and started in. "I have something to tell you. When I thought I had lost you … it was horrible, as if life had ended for me too. I can't hold it back any longer. I love you."

Regret flooded his eyes and he squeezed his hand in hers. "I love you too, but I'm going back to Afghanistan. I can't ask you to wait for me, not knowing what's ahead, what could happen." He swallowed. "I had a friend, Lee Bordman. You may remember him."

She nodded and waited silently, knowing this was important to him and that if they were to have the relationship they both wanted, she needed to understand how he felt about leaving a woman behind. She also knew in spite of whatever he said, she would wait. The way she felt about him was too important to ignore. God had given him to her, and she belonged with him. Nothing could change that.

"I was in the vehicle behind him when a roadside bomb exploded. He was killed."

"I'd heard about that."

"What you may not know is he had a newborn son he'd never seen. He was so proud of that baby—looking forward to seeing him. That's all he talked about. Now that boy will never know his father."

"That's terrible, Blake. I can't imagine what that must have been like. But what does it have to do with us?"

"I went to see his wife after I got home. I'll never forget the way she looked, the things she said. I came away knowing I could never put a woman I loved through that."

She stared at him. "What are you trying to say?"

He licked his lips. "I'm saying I can't marry you and then leave you behind, not knowing if I'll come back or not."

Carley leaned forward, resting her elbows on the bed. "Listen to me, Blake. Whatever happens, I'll be here waiting. I love you and you love me, and nothing's going to change that."

He started to speak and she put her hand over his mouth. "Hear me out. If something happens to you, the results for me will be the same, whether we're married or not. I'll still grieve. It's too late to change that. The question is, do you really want to marry me?"

"More than anything, but—"

"Then give love a chance." Carley firmed her lips. Strength from somewhere—from God—surged through her. "You don't have to ask. You don't have a choice. I'm not about to let you get away. I'll wait, I'll pray, and you had better understand one thing—you belong to me, and we belong together, no matter what the future holds."

Russ spoke from the doorway. "You'd better take her up on that. You're not likely to get a better offer."

Blake grinned. "Am I arguing? I can't think of anything I'd like more."

"You're a lucky man."

Carley shook her head. "You're doing it again, talking about me like I'm not here."

Blake looked up at her. "What do you want me to do?"

"Well, you could start with kissing me."

When they looked up, it was just the two of them. After a moment of silence, Blake smiled. "You're something else, you know that? All right, you win. I love you, Carley Sutherland. Will you marry me?"

She reached out to caress his cheek. "Oh, yes. You know I will. Right away—before you leave. I'll start making plans."

"Keep them simple, okay?"

"Simple and beautiful. You'll see."

And they sealed it with a kiss.

The day of their wedding dawned with sunshine and a clear blue sky. Carley remembered what her mother always said—an old saying, but today it fit. "Happy the bride the sun shines on."

Yes, she was happy, gloriously so. Blake would be leaving soon and she'd be here without him, but they would be bound together by love and in the sight of God. She wished her parents could have been here, but she knew they would be with her in her memories. At last she could think of them without being burdened with guilt. God had taken that away from her, and she was free.

Kurt was in the hospital under armed guard, recovering from a chest wound, and Mr. Quigley was in jail, charged with taking part in attempted murder and harboring a fugitive.

At a quarter after nine, Kara pulled into the driveway. She came in and helped gather Carley's gown and accessories. The flowers would be delivered at the church. After they were in the car, Kara looked over at her and grinned. "Are you nervous?"

"No, not at all. I thought I would be, but all I can think of is that I'm marrying the man of my dreams."

They entered the church, going to the classroom set aside for the bride and bridesmaids to dress. Kara slipped the garment bag off Carley's gown and helped her into it before donning her own maid of honor gown of blue silk.

Carley faced the full-length mirror. The gown of white silk and lace fell around her in folds. Her blond hair waved down to brush her shoulders. For the first time, she felt a nervous tremor. The church was full and everyone would be watching.

The opening notes of the organ sounded, and she mounted the stairs to the foyer where Russ was waiting to walk her to the front. He smiled down at her. "You ready?"

Carley nodded and they began walking slowly down the aisle to where Blake waited for her. At that moment, she had eyes only for him. Nothing else mattered. He held out his hand and she reached to take it, his touch warm and intimate.

Pastor Rick Sanders began the ceremony. "Dearly beloved, we are gathered here to celebrate the marriage of Carley and Blake. A wedding is a celebration of love. Corinthians One says that love is patient and kind. It is not jealous or boastful, not irritable or resentful, not arrogant or rude. Love doesn't insist on its own way. It does not rejoice in the wrong, but rejoices in the right. Love bears all things, believes all things, hopes in all things, and endures all things. Love never ends. Today, we meet to rejoice in Blake and Carley's commitment to that love."

Carley glanced at Blake to find him gazing down at her, his eyes shining with love. Her heart skipped a beat as she smiled at him.

Pastor Rick continued. "Do you, Blake, take this woman to be your lawfully wedded wife?"

Blake's voice came out husky but firm. "I do."

Then it was her turn. "Do you, Carley, take this man as your lawfully wedded husband?"

"I do." The words gushed out.

They slipped the rings on each other's fingers. Then came the moment she had been waiting for.

"You may kiss the bride."

Carley moved into Blake's arms. His lips met hers, soft, tender, and loving. When they parted, he looked deeply into her eyes. "I love you, Mrs. Richards."

She smiled, her heart melting. "I love you too."

Blake kissed Carley again, and for her, the church and congregation disappeared. In her mind, she pictured a flowing green meadow where she and Blake strolled, all alone—just the two of them.

It would be that way from then on. Whether he was home or on the battlefield, they would be together in their hearts. No matter what the future held, she knew that they would make it through as one, because they had already triumphed over so much and were bonded in love.

Together forever.

She liked the sound of that.

Made in the USA
Columbia, SC
13 September 2017